JUST PEACHY

Jean Ure

HarperCollins *Children's Books*

First published in Great Britain by HarperCollins *Children's Books* in 2013
HarperCollins *Children's Books* is a division of HarperCollins*Publishers* Ltd,
77–85 Fulham Palace Road, Hammersmith, London, W6 8JB.

www.harpercollins.co.uk

www.jeanure.com

1

Just Peachy
Text © Jean Ure 2013
Illustrations © HarperCollins *Publishers* 2013

The author and illustrator assert the moral right to be identified as the author
and illustrator of this work.

ISBN 978-0-00-751568-4

Typeset by Palimpsest Book Production Ltd,
Falkirk, Stirlingshire
Printed and bound in England by Clays Ltd, St Ives plc.

MIX
Paper from
responsible sources
FSC www.fsc.org **FSC C007454**

To Lottie Erratt-Rose

CHAPTER ONE

I never knew until recently that it is a criminal offence to shout "Fire!" in a crowded theatre. Well, or a crowded anywhere, I suppose, if it comes to that. Unless of course there actually *is* a fire, in which case you should probably shout just as loudly as you possibly can, at the top of your lungs, like, **"FIRE!"** It's just if there isn't one that it's criminal, I guess because you could cause panic and start a stampede, and people could get trampled on or even crushed to death, and then it would be all your fault and you could be sent to prison.

I was at the dentist when I made this discovery. Sitting there with Mum, reading a magazine and trying to take my mind off the horrors to come. I am a bit of a wimp about the dentist. Mum knows this, so I think she was quite surprised when I gave this little bark of bitter laughter, like, "Huh!"

She said, "And what have you found that's so amusing?"

Well, obviously it wasn't the idea of people being crushed to death. But all the same it did strike me as funny, cos quite honestly, with my family, you could bawl through a megaphone at a thousand decibels and it wouldn't cause panic. Nobody would stampede. They wouldn't even bother to look up.

I know this, cos I have tried it. Last year, in the Star

of Bengal, which is Dad's favourite Indian restaurant. Saturday evening it was, and we'd all gone out to have a meal. Mum and Dad, my sister Charlotte, my brother Cooper, me and the twins. I was eleven at the time. Charlie was thirteen, Coop fourteen and Fergus and Flora had just had their ninth birthday. They were all sitting there, airing their views and shouting at one another across the table, making a lot of noise, same as they always do. It's something they can't seem to help; it is just the way they are.

"Naturally exuberant," Mum says, with a touch of pride.

They all have these massive great personalities, the sort that come roaring at you like tidal waves, and they all have *opinions*. Opinions about anything and everything. Sometimes quite violent ones. Even the twins.

"We're just a very lively bunch," chortles Mum.

Except for me, who is probably a bit of a disappointment. I do *have* opinions, but I find I don't voice them all that often. Not, at any rate, when I'm with the rest of the family. When I'm with the family I mostly just sit quite quietly, like a mouse.

It was what I was doing that evening while the conversation rocketed to and fro, with Dad yelling at Coop, Charlie yelling at Mum, the twins yelling at each other. I expect to outsiders it might have sounded like they were fighting, but they never fight. They are all very good-natured. It is just that yelling happens to be the everyday mode of expression in my family. If there is anything you want to say, you have to join in and start yelling yourself to get their attention.

Which, in the end, is what I did. I would far rather just have gone on quietly sitting there, doing my mouse act, keeping myself to myself, but I knew that the time had come. I had to take action. I had to rise up and shout "Fire!"

Well, to be honest I didn't actually shout, cos I mean we were sitting in a crowded restaurant and it would have been rude. Unlike the rest of my family, I do try to have *some* manners. And I didn't actually use the word fire, for the same reason: crowded restaurant. I wouldn't have wanted to frighten people. (Or to commit a criminal offence, though I didn't realise then that it was one.) But the thing that I said – that I *tried* to say – in this very firm, clear voice, was something Mum and Dad would have found every bit as startling. If they'd stopped yelling long enough to listen.

I got as far as, "Actually—"

And then Mum came crashing in over the top.

"Darling," she shrieked, "that's wonderful!"

Needless to say, she wasn't talking to me. She was talking to Charlie.

"It's one of the main parts," yelled Charlie.

"Darling, I know!" Mum reached out and squeezed her hand. "I'm so proud of you!"

I sank back on my chair. Obviously *not* the right moment for an earth-shattering announcement.

"Alastair, did you hear that?" cried Mum, leaning forward to rap Dad on the back of the hand with a menu.

"What's that?" said Dad.

"Your clever daughter's playing Gwendolen!"

"And your clever son," said Coop, "is writing the music."

"Music?" Dad seemed puzzled. "I thought it was a play?"

Mum and Charlie exchanged pitying glances. Coop rolled his eyes.

"Dad," wailed Charlie, "we already told you... it's being turned into a musical!"

"By none other than yours truly," added Coop.

"Is that so? In that case—" Dad thumped triumphantly on the table, causing all the cutlery to bounce. Being on the radio, he is very into the whole showbiz thing – "this calls for a celebration!"

Definitely not the moment.

"Such a talented family," beamed Dad.

"Yes, and that's not all," said Mum. "Tell him, you two!"

"Me and Flora's gonna be in *our* play too," said Fergus. "Dunno what parts we're doing, but we're def'nitely gonna be in it. Miss Marshall said so."

"Course you're going to be in it," said Dad. "Course you are! Can't put on a play without a McBride in the cast!"

Mum smiled fondly. "Imagine," she said, "when the twins get to Summerfield that will make four of them! Well, five, of course, with Peachy." She hastily patted me on the shoulder. Mum doesn't like me to feel left out. She does her best to include me whenever she remembers. "But four in the limelight!" She giggled. "A clutch of McBrides!"

I wouldn't actually mind being in the limelight. Being on stage. Having my name in the programme. Not that I exactly hanker after it. I'm just saying that I wouldn't mind. I don't have stage fright or anything. But I've come to the conclusion that there are backstage people and there are onstage people, and

I'm just one of the backstage ones. Least, that's what my family would say.

"Hey! Will I still be around?" said Coop.

"What, when the twins go there? Of course you will! It's only two years away."

Two years for the twins, just a few months for me. I was supposed to be starting next term. They'd had all our names down for Summerfield practically ever since we were born. It's like a sort of family tradition. On Dad's side, that is.

I took a breath. It was time I dropped my bombshell.

"*Actually*—"

"You never know," said Coop, "I might be at music college by then."

"Not at the age of sixteen," said Mum.

"Not even if I'm a genius?"

"You are a genius, darling, but you're still staying on at school. I cannot possibly have you leaving till the twins are there. Imagine," exulted Mum, "a whole dynasty. A McBride takeover!"

I cleared my throat. Noisily.

"*ACTUALLY…*" I said. I leaned forward. "I d—"

"Five, all at once!"

"I don't—"

"Five's not the record," said Dad. "When I was a boy, there were six of us at one time. Your Uncle Daniel – " he nodded at us as he ticked names off on his fingers – "your Aunt Helen, me, plus three cousins: Will, Shula, Rory. All there at the same time!"

Mum said, "Yes, but this will be five from just one family. I bet that's never happened before! We ought to ask for reduced rates."

My heart began hammering. This was it! I had to get it out. *Now.* Before they went rushing off to demand reductions.

I took another breath. Deeper this time.

"As a matter of fact," I said, "I don't really—"

"Bubbly!" Dad thumped again, on the table. "A bottle of bubbly. That's what we need!"

"Don't really w—"

"McBrides United!"

"—really want to go to Summerfield!"

I might just as well not have bothered. Nobody was listening.

"What a team, eh?" Dad winked at Mum.

"We are doing rather well," agreed Mum.

"Yeah, cos me and Flora – " Fergus bounced boastfully on his chair – "we didn't even have to take auditions! Everybody else did, but not us."

"That's right." Flora nodded. "Miss Marshall said she knew what we were capable of."

"Well, of course she did," said Dad. "Chips off the old block, the pair of you!"

I think what he meant was, they took after him. Well, and after Mum too, if it comes to that. Mum might not be on the radio, but she is every bit as theatrical as Dad. So are all the others. They are all chips off the old block. Except for me. I am like the cuckoo in the nest. The odd one out. It wouldn't ever have occurred to Miss Marshall to say she knew what

I was capable of. She didn't even suggest I took the audition, even though I can sing in tune. Of course I could have asked her, if I'd really wanted. But I kept thinking how she'd look at me, with this air of doubt.

"You, Peaches? I thought you'd be helping out backstage?"

What I would have liked was for her to ask *me*. But even if she had I probably wouldn't have been given anything, and then the twins would have told Mum, and Mum would have made a big fuss and hugged me and cried, "Oh, darling, don't think you have to compete! You have your own thing."

It was like a sort of family myth, me having my own thing. Nobody ever said what it was, and I never quite liked to ask. It was just something Mum used to say to try and make me feel good.

"I'll tell you what!" Mum's voice rang out, very clear and bell-like. Heads at the next table turned to stare. "If I hadn't had you lot, I might have gone onstage myself."

Dad at once started to sing. He has a deep dark baritone. Very *loud*.

"*Don't put your daughter on the stage, Mrs Worthington—*"

Mum slapped at him. "I could have done!"

"Of course you could, my angel." Dad blew her a kiss across the table. "You could have done anything you wanted."

"Instead of which, I had this lot."

"Ah, but think how proud they're going to make you!"

"What I should *like* to think," said Mum, "is that we could get a reduction in school fees. Dog breeders get reductions. Why can't we? I mean, let's face it, sending five of them…"

I think at this point I must have made a little squeak of protest without realising it. Mum broke off and looked at me.

"Did you say something, darling?"

I opened my mouth. *I don't want to go to Summerfield!*

I'd been trying to say it for the last fifteen minutes. And now, just as I was on the point of actually doing so, Dad gave a joyful cry – "Here's Raj!" – and Mum snatched up a menu and instructed everyone to order. The moment had passed.

"What'll we have? Who wants what?"

"Poppadoms, anyone? Who's for poppadoms?"

And then they all started shouting at once.

"Chicken tikka!"

"Prawn masala!"

"Lamb biryani!"

Raj, who was used to us, stood calmly in the midst of it all writing things down.

"Everyone ordered?" said Mum brightly.

"Yes, yes." Dad, impatient, gathered up the menus. "Don't forget the bubbly!"

It was Raj who noticed I hadn't ordered anything.

"And for the young lady?" he said.

"Young lady?" said Mum. "Which young lady?"

"Just Peachy," said Coop.

"What? She hasn't ordered?"

I'm not absolutely positive, but I *think* Raj may have winked at me. Sort of like showing sympathy. My family!

"So what are you going to have?" said Mum. "If you had the chicken korma, we could mix and match."

"Yes, all right," I said.

"You're sure?"

I nodded. Raj stood gravely, his pen poised.

"She'll have the chicken korma," said Mum. "Honestly, darling, you really must learn to speak up!"

"Like on stage," said Flora. "If you don't **SPEAK UP** – " her voice rose to a shriek – "no one'll be able to hear you."

"Well, they'll certainly be able to hear you, all right," said Mum.

Flora gave this little complacent smirk. "That's why Miss Marshall chose us, cos we have these really **BIG** voices. There's this one girl in our class – Alisha Briggs? She really fancies herself, she thinks she's going to get to play the lead, but she won't cos she has this silly little squeaky voice like an ant. Squeaky squeaky!"

"Ants don't squeak," I said.

"They do so," said Flora. "You just can't hear them. Like you can't hear Alisha. Plus she can't even sing in tune. She goes like this: doh, re, mi-i-i-..."

Flora's voice rose, shrill and quavery. One of the ladies at the next table placed a hand over her ear.

"I'm going to be singing," said Charlie. "Coop's already written one of my songs for me. Haven't you?"

"Right," said Coop. "Wanna give them a taste of it?"

Charlie never needs a second invitation. To be fair she does actually have a good voice. Very high and silvery. Not always quite in tune, but who cares?

"Lovely, lovely!" cried Mum, when we'd listened to three full verses plus the chorus. Everyone clapped, madly. Dad even shouted, "Bravo!" I was a bit embarrassed so I just tapped my hands together without making any sound, but some people in the restaurant actually turned in their seats and joined in. Even the lady at the next table, the one who'd put her hand over her ear.

I'm always surprised that people don't get angry and ask us to be quiet, but they never seem to. I suspect it's cos of Dad being on the radio, and sometimes on TV, which makes him a sort of mini celeb. Celebs can get away with anything. I bet if ordinary people were to start singing and shouting and making a noise, Raj would say something quickly enough, but he was smiling happily as he brought the champagne. Of course, Dad spends a *lot* of money in his restaurant. I expect that helps.

"Someone's birthday?" said Raj, as he popped the cork.

"Celebration," said Dad. "Double whammy."

Mum explained about Charlie and Coop and the twins.

"All reaching for the stars!"

This time, Raj really did wink at me. It gave me this little glow of happiness. It made me feel that he was on my side. Everybody, but everybody, loves Mum and Dad, cos they are funny and warm and they make people laugh. But maybe Raj understood how it was, being me. Just Peachy, the mouse in the middle.

"Righty-o!" Dad raised his glass. "Let us have a toast... the McBrides!"

When we'd toasted the whole family together we toasted Charlie and Coop, and after that we toasted the twins. And then Mum said, "To Peachy!" and they all drank a toast to me. And then the food came and everyone immediately fell on it in a kind of mad feeding frenzy, like in those wildlife films where they show bunches of jackals tearing some poor dead thing to shreds. You have to eat really, really fast if you want to keep up. Sometimes I manage it OK, but sometimes I am a bit slow. What made me slow that particular evening was worrying about how and when I was going to break my earth-shattering news to Mum and Dad and how they were going to react. They were not going to be happy.

"Peachy," said Mum, "stop messing your food about."

"What's the matter?" said Dad. "Don't you want it?" He leaned across and dug his fork into a piece of chicken. The very piece I'd been about to dig my fork into.

"Oh, well, if she's not going to eat it," said Mum, and she leaned across and dug her fork in too.

"Really," said Dad, "I don't know why you order things if you don't like them."

"If you'd have preferred something else," said Mum, "you only had to say."

"No need to be scared." Dad helped himself to more chicken. "Just sing right out!"

"She can't sing," said Flora.

I said, "I can so! Shows how much you know."

Complacently, chewing chicken, Dad said, "All the McBrides can sing. Even Peachy."

Tomorrow I would *definitely* tell them.

CHAPTER TWO

Usually on a Sunday morning I stay curled up under the duvet for as long as I possibly can. All the family does, except for Mum. Mum is always the first up. She says she likes to have the house to herself for half an hour before the rest of us appear and start banging and clattering.

"A little bit of peace and quiet, that's all I ask."

Hah! That is a joke. Even when she does have the house to herself Mum isn't quiet. *Or* peaceful. I could hear her, that Sunday, down in the kitchen bawling at the radio. I knew I had to make an effort. Catch her on her own.

Blearily, I forced my eyes open and with one hand threw off the duvet. The hand immediately fell back with a heavy *flump* on to the bed. It felt like a bag of wet cement. My eyes started to close again. It was a great temptation just to let them. I *so* didn't want to have to drop my bombshell!

An angry bellow from the kitchen jerked me back into wakefulness. I swung my legs over the side of the bed, groped my way into jeans and T-shirt, wobbled out on to the landing and staggered downstairs and along the hall.

Mum was sitting with her feet on the kitchen table, drinking a cup of coffee and shouting at the radio. Everyone in my family always shouts at the radio. They can't ever listen to anything without joining in. What Mum was listening to were the Sunday-morning highlights of Dad's weekday breakfast show, when Dad gives his opinion about what is happening in the world and the public call in and give theirs, and they have a conversation about it. Well, sometimes they do. Sometimes Dad decides that people are idiots and cuts them off. Sometimes they decide that Dad is an idiot and cut themselves off. Sometimes some of them are bonkers. Like this one woman, Monica, that calls in practically every day. She was on there now, her words splattering round the kitchen like machine-gun fire.

"If-you-ask-me-they-should-all-be-made-to-run-naked-through-the-streets-and-have-raw-sewage-thrown-at-them."

I giggled. I loved Monica! "What's she talking about?"

"Politicians," said Mum. "Oh, listen to her, listen to her! That is too much. She is completely mad! JUST BE QUIET, WOMAN, AND GO AWAY! Honestly, I don't know why your dad puts up with it."

"He probably agrees with her," I said. "He probably thinks it's a good idea."

"What? Naked politicians running through the streets?" Mum rolled her eyes. "Heaven forbid! They're quite bad enough with their clothes *on*, thank you very much. What are you doing up so bright and early?"

This was it. The moment I was dreading. I sank down on to a chair opposite her.

"Mum," I said, "there's something I w—"

"Omigod, there she goes again! Get rid of her, get rid of her!"

"OK." I leaned over and switched the radio off. Mum gave a shriek.

"What are you doing?"

"You said to get rid of her."

"I was talking to your dad! I didn't mean – oh, never mind, it doesn't matter. I lose all patience with that woman. Did you want to say something?"

She'd noticed. At last! I braced myself against the table.

"You know last night," I said, "when you were saying how there'd be five of us at Summerfield?"

"Yes! Great fun. But I definitely intend to ask about a reduction."

"The thing is," I said, "I—" I stopped. I couldn't get it out!

"You what?" said Mum.

I gulped. "I don't want to go there!"

My voice came out in a pathetic squeak. Mum stared, like I had suddenly gone green or turned into some weird kind of *thing* from outer space.

"You don't want to go to Summerfield?"

I hung my head.

"You're not serious?" said Mum. "Please! Tell me you're not serious?"

I took a deep, trembling breath.

"Omigod," cried Mum, "you are!"

There was a silence. Long, and awkward. Mum ran a despairing hand through her hair. Mum's hair is very thick and springy. It was already sticking up from where she'd been sleeping on it. Now she'd made it look like a bird's nest.

"I'm really sorry," I whispered.

This was turning out even worse than I'd thought. I had never, ever known Mum be at a loss for words before. She was shaking her head, like she had earwigs crawling in her ears. She seemed totally bewildered.

"Darling," she said, "what on earth are you talking about? Of course you're going there! The McBrides always go to Summerfield. It's all arranged!"

"Yes," I said. "I know."

"Coop and Charlie couldn't be happier. They love it!"

"Yes," I said. "I know they do."

"It's not like you'll be on your own. They'll be there to keep an eye on you."

I stared down at the table.

"And the twins," said Mum. "They can't wait to get there!"

I mumbled again that I was sorry.

"Is it something someone's said? Something that's put you off?"

I assured her that it wasn't.

"So... what is it?" said Mum. "I don't understand! Why all of a sudden don't you want to go?"

"I just don't!"

The squeak had turned into a kind of desperate wail. Please don't keep asking me! Because how could I explain? How could I tell Mum the reason I didn't want to go to Summerfield was that I needed to be on my own? To be somewhere I could just be *me*, safely anonymous, without everyone knowing my dad was on the radio and who my brothers and sisters were. I loved my family, I truly did, but sometimes they made me wonder whether I actually really existed or whether I was just this empty space in their midst.

"Darling?" A new idea had obviously struck Mum. She studied me anxiously. "It's not *because* of them, is it? Charlie and Coop? Because they're both doing so well? It's not that that's bothering you? Because it really shouldn't! I mean, Coop and his music... we can't any of us compete with Coop. Not even your dad. As for Charlie – well! She's just being Charlie. Centre of attention. That's her thing, it's what she does. Not everyone can be like Charlie. We're all different! And just as well, if you ask me. The world would be a very boring place if we were all the same, don't you think?"

Mum gave me this bright, hopeful smile, like begging me to agree with her. I smiled rather tremulously back, but was saved from having to say anything by the whirlwind arrival of Dad, who came crashing noisily through the door. Dad is quite a *large* person; he does a lot of crashing.

Mum said, "Alastair, we need to t—"

She never got to finish the sentence. With a howl, Dad lunged at the radio.

"Why isn't this on? Why aren't we listening to my highlights?"

"I was," said Mum. "Peachy turned it off. We n—"

But Dad had already switched the radio back on.

His rich fruity tones came booming out across the kitchen.

"Hah!" he said. "I knew they'd play this bit!"

Mum pulled a face. I sort of sympathised with her. Dad does tend to drown people out. But then Mum does a fair bit of drowning herself.

"This next guy was a right plonker," said Dad. "How about mad Monica? Did they play her?"

"Never mind mad Monica," said Mum rather grimly. "We have a problem on our hands."

"Really?" Dad helped himself to a cup of coffee. "What's that?"

"Just Peachy," said Mum. "She doesn't want to go to Summerfield."

"*What?*"

"You heard me," said Mum. "She doesn't want to go to—"

"Oh, for God's sake," yelled Dad, "kill that damn radio!"

For the second time, I leaned across and turned it off.

"What do you mean, she doesn't want to go to Summerfield?"

"What I said. She doesn't want to go there."

If I'd thought Mum's reaction was bad, Dad's was a thousand times worse. It was like his mouth opened and a bomb exploded, shooting words all over the kitchen. They bounced off the walls, banged against the windows. Mum waited patiently, drinking her coffee. I sat hunched on my chair, feet on the rung, elbows on table, chin propped in hands, my face covered. You can't interrupt Dad when he is in full flow; you just have to take shelter until the storm has passed. As soon as it has, Dad becomes calm again. His temper is massive, but it usually dies down as quickly as it flares up.

Mum said, "Right! Can we talk now?"

"We'd better," said Dad.

"If you'll just stop moving about and sit yourself down."

"I am sitting down," said Dad. He pulled out a chair. "I'm in a state of shock. What is all this nonsense?"

Mum said that unfortunately she didn't think it was nonsense. "I think she's serious... she doesn't want to go there."

"I got that bit," said Dad. "What I want to know is why?"

"I think," said Mum, "it's because she feels scared of being overshadowed by Charlie and Coop. What with Charlie hogging all the limelight and Coop being some kind of prodigy – and then, of course, there's the twins, when they come along. They're not exactly shrinking violets, bless them!"

Dad said, "You can say that again." He gave one of his throaty chuckles. "Talk about a double act!"

"Exactly," said Mum. "You can understand if she feels a bit overwhelmed."

They were going on about me like I was deaf, or in another room. They did that sometimes. Just stopped noticing that I was there.

"I don't think we should push her, if she really doesn't want to. I would hate her to end up with some kind of complex."

"It is the curse of coming from a gifted family," agreed Dad. "There's bound to be a bit of…" He waved a hand. "Well! A bit of… you know. Difficulty."

"Although she does have her own thing. Just because it's not showy doesn't mean it's not as valid."

"All the same." Dad slurped his coffee. "Hard act to follow."

"Very hard," said Mum.

"So! What do we do?"

There was a pause. I waited for Mum to say something but she just sat there, munching her top lip.

"*Well?*" Dad was getting worked up again. He slapped his hand on the table. "Say something!"

Since it seemed that Mum wasn't going to, I thought that perhaps I should.

"You could always send me somewhere else," I said.

Their heads snapped round, like, *Ooh, she's there! She's been there all the time!*

"We could." Mum said it slowly, considering the idea. "But where would we send you?"

"That," said Dad, "is the question."

Eagerly I leaned forward. I'd been doing a lot of thinking about where I'd like to go. "What about Winterbourne?" I said.

"Oh, darling, no!" Mum gave a little shudder. "Not Winterbourne! You'd be completely lost. You'd never survive! It's far too big. And anyway, it doesn't have a good reputation at all."

I didn't care that it was big. I didn't care about its reputation. All that interested me was that Winterbourne High was just about as far as you could possibly get from somewhere like Summerfield. Nobody would know me. Nobody would know my family. I could just be *me*.

"It's only down the road," I pleaded. "I could walk there!"

"But why would you want to?" said Dad. He seemed genuinely puzzled. Why would anyone in their right senses choose Winterbourne High over Summerfield? "Give me one good reason!"

"You wouldn't have to pay for me?" I suggested.

Dad gave an angry roar. "Don't you try pulling that one, my girl! There's a little thing called equality in this house, yes? If we pay for the others, we pay for you. You'll have to come up with something a bit better than that!"

"I like the uniform?" I said.

"Darling, it's *grey*," said Mum. Summerfield's is bright red. Far more to Mum's taste.

I said, "I like grey."

"Nonsense!" said Mum.

"Rubbish!" said Dad.

"It wouldn't suit you at *all*," said Mum. "You need a bit of colour. Something bright. Put you in grey, you'd just fade into the background."

"Not," said Dad, "that one chooses a school by its uniform."

"Well, no, of course. Absolutely not! But I don't think it helps if it makes one look a total fright. And you know, darling, you do need all the help you can get. You don't want to *fade*. How about Sacred Heart? That's a nice school!"

"They wear kilts," I said.

"I know. So sweet! That blue would really suit you. Bring out the colour of your eyes. Of course — " a note of doubt crept into Mum's voice — "it is all girls. I'm never too sure about that. On the other hand, you do have brothers, so maybe it wouldn't matter too much." Mum turned enthusiastically to Dad. "Do you know, I really think Sacred Heart would be a good choice!"

"Bring out the colour of her eyes," said Dad sarcastically.

"Oh, don't be silly! That's neither here nor there," said Mum. "I was just thinking how it was exactly the sort of school that would suit her… small classes, no pressure… no one to compete with. And all those lovely nuns! Let's check out their website."

It seemed that my fate was sealed.

"We are assuming," said Dad, "that they can take her."

"Oh, I'm sure they will," said Mum.

Mum is always sure about everything, and it has to be said, she is usually right. She has this gift of bending people to her will.

"Just leave it to me," she said.

She broke the news to the others later that day when we all went up the road for Sunday lunch.

"Everybody! A little bit of hush," she said. "Hot news!"

"About what?" said Coop. "Dad's won another radio award?"

"I wish!" said Dad.

"Right," said Charlie, "cos you've only got about a dozen of them."

"Can't have too many."

"Will you please HUSH?" said Mum. "There's something I have to tell you."

"Ooh!" Coop gave a little shiver. "Sounds important!"

"Not desperately," said Dad. "It's just Peachy."

Dad was still quite cross. And nobody else cared all that much. There wasn't any reason they should. Like Dad said, it wasn't really important. Not like Dad getting a radio award, or Charlie getting a lead in the school play. Just Peachy, being silly and awkward.

Mum patted my hand. "Don't worry," she said. "Your dad will get over it. And I do actually think you'll be far better off on your own. There won't be all that stress of trying to keep up; you can just quietly concentrate on doing your own thing. I'm so glad I thought of it!"

CHAPTER THREE

"...just a bit insecure, which isn't really surprising, I suppose, when you come to think about it."

The voice was Mum's. She was speaking to someone on the phone. Who? I wondered. And who was she talking about?

"The others are doing almost frighteningly well."

I froze, in the hall on the other side of the door. I hadn't meant to eavesdrop but I couldn't help hearing. Mum's voice is very clear and penetrating.

"All that high-flying. Enough to make anyone insecure." She gave a little tinkle of laughter. "Even me!"

Who? *Who?* Who was she talking about? I hovered guiltily, unable to tear myself away.

"I don't think I'd say she was jealous," said Mum. "A bit envious perhaps – which is only to be expected. More a sense of... not being able to compete? Which you can perfectly understand. It all just comes so easily to the rest of them."

She was talking about me. I knew she was. But who was she talking *to?*

"Oh, yes, much better," said Mum. "Far happier now she's at Sacred Heart. I always felt that Summerfield wouldn't be quite right for her. An excellent school – the others just love it – but—" Mum broke off as I pushed open the door. "Ah, Peachy!" she said. "Do you want a word with Big Gran?"

Big Gran is Dad's mum. She is quite a large person, like Dad, but unlike Dad she is not a bully. Dad is known for being a bully. He was once called the rudest man on the radio. Big Gran is quite sweet. She has always tried really hard to make me feel good about myself. Sometimes she tries a bit *too* hard, and then it is embarrassing. But I know she means well.

I said, "Hi, Gran."

Gran said, "Hello, sweetheart! I'm so glad to hear you're getting on all right at your new school. It's a pity about Summerfield, but don't let it bother you. I mean, your dad being upset and all that. He'll get over it. What's important is that you should never be made to feel you have to do things simply because your brothers and sisters do them. You just concentrate on being your own person."

It was what Gran was always telling me to do. I promised her that I was concentrating like mad.

"Good," said Gran. "That's good. Always remember that simply because something's right for the others doesn't necessarily mean it's right for you. You mustn't let yourself be put under any pressure."

I assured her that I wouldn't.

"Well, I certainly hope not," said Gran. "It's not as if you're in competition. I know it can be difficult at times. I've been there! I'll never forget the day your dad's Auntie Esther got into the Royal Ballet School."

Auntie Esther is Gran's sister. She was a famous ballet dancer in her time.

"Oh, such a to-do!" said Gran. "Big, big celebration! WELL DONE, ESTHER! Huge great banner, special cake in the shape of a ballet shoe, all over the local paper, called up on stage in morning assembly… Oh, dear, I was so jealous I can't tell you! Not that I had any ambitions in that direction. At my size?" Gran laughed. A rich, fruity laugh like Dad's. "Forget it! But I wouldn't have minded some of the attention, I don't mind admitting. It was a bit of a rough time. Dear little Esther, so dainty and talented, and great lumping Elinor who couldn't even walk into a room without tripping over her size-seven feet. But then, you see, we both grew up and I did my own thing and couldn't have been happier. So it just goes to show, doesn't it?"

I made a vague mumbling sound of agreement.

"That's the spirit!" said Gran. "Now——" she settled down for a cosy chat. "Tell me a bit more about this new school. Sacred Heart. I don't know it. What is it like?"

"It's all right," I said.

"You mean, really all right? Or just *all right, not bad?*"

I said, "Really all right. Really!"

I'd been at Sacred Heart for over a fortnight now. I hadn't been too sure at first. I'd wanted to go to Winterbourne because Winterbourne was huge. Nearly 1,500 pupils. Enough to swallow me up and keep me safely anonymous. Sacred Heart was hardly any bigger than primary school, where I hadn't been anonymous *at all.* Everybody had known who my dad was. Everybody could remember Charlie and Coop. Everybody knew the twins. And everybody, but everybody, was always expecting me to be just as high-powered and talented as they were. Until they discovered that I wasn't, and then it was like, "Oh, that's just Peachy. She's not a bit like her sister."

So just at the beginning, when I started at Sacred Heart, I was really anxious, because suppose someone discovered about Dad, or knew someone who knew Charlie or Coop? In the whole of Year 7 there were only thirty people. Once one person found out, everybody would know, and I might just as well have gone to Summerfield and not caused Dad all that grief. Cos he was still a bit cross about it, even now.

On our very first day, Mrs Bradbeer, our class teacher, said she wanted us all to introduce ourselves.

"Most of you have come up from the junior school together, but some of you are new, so I'd like everybody to say a few words about themselves, and about their family, just to break the ice. All right?"

No! I cringed, trying to hide behind the person in front. This was like my worst nightmare come true.

Mrs Bradbeer obviously saw the panic on my face. She said, "Try not to look so worried, Peaches!"

Peaches? Heads snapped round. The whole class stared. I felt like digging a hole and burying myself. Trust Mum! Peaches had been her choice. She couldn't just pick something ordinary and unremarkable like Amy or Emma. Oh, no! She had to go for something that would make everyone turn and stare.

Mrs Bradbeer smiled reassuringly. "You don't have to say more than you feel comfortable with. Just a few words will do. Zoe, why don't you get us started?"

Zoe was one of the ones that had come up from Juniors. Full of self-importance, she pushed back her chair and bounced to her feet. You could tell she was someone that just loved the sound of her own voice. In loud, ringing tones she announced that she was Zoe Kingman and that her big ambition was to be successful and make a lot of money. She said she had a dad that was an architect and a mum that was "in the City".

"Like she's really high up in one of the big banks,

only I'd better not say which one cos of people getting jealous and thinking she's probably making too much money, which Mum says is just the politics of envy. I personally think that if you work hard you deserve to make lots of money; I don't see anything wrong in it. At any rate," said Zoe, "that is what I am going to do."

She sat back down with a self-satisfied *flump*. I noticed that the girl next to me was pulling a face. I felt a bit like pulling one myself but I wasn't quite brave enough. Several people were nodding, and one girl even started to clap.

Mrs Bradbeer said, "Thank you, Zoe. That's got the ball rolling. Lola? You next?"

One by one, everybody got up and told us about themselves. They all seemed to have mums and dads that were doctors, or solicitors, or bank managers. I waited for someone to say her dad was a butcher, or her mum was a cleaning lady, but it didn't happen. I sat glumly, hunched at my desk, wishing I was at Winterbourne instead of having to sit here listening as people went gabbing on about themselves and their hugely important parents. I didn't think anyone at Winterbourne would really care what other people's mums and dads did. I certainly wasn't going to tell them anything about mine!

Mrs Bradbeer was going round the class at random. She seemed to be leaving me till last. Maybe, with any luck, the bell would ring and I wouldn't have to do it.

"Millie?" said Mrs Bradbeer. "Shall we hear from you?"

The girl next to me sprang up.

"Millie O'Dowd," she said. "One mum, one dad, three annoying little sisters. My mum's called Sinead, my dad's called Kevin, and my sisters are the Diddy People. Well, that's what I call them. Dunno what else to say, really. Oh, except my mum's a school dinner lady and my dad's on the buses, only I'd better not say which one cos of people getting jealous and thinking bus drivers are greedy when they want more money."

Someone gave a little titter. Mrs Bradbeer put a warning finger to her lips.

"That's about it really," said Millie. "I haven't yet decided what my big ambition is, but hopefully I'll end up a millionaire."

This time lots of people tittered. Mrs Bradbeer said, "Thank you very much, Millie. Short and sweet and very pointed."

Millie grinned at me again as she sat down. It was an impish sort of grin, like, '*I enjoyed that!*' An uncertain silence had settled over the room. I could almost see people wrestling with the idea that someone should have a mum that was a dinner lady and a dad that was on the buses. I felt suddenly bold, and gave Millie a big grin in return. She mouthed at me: "You in a minute!"

I was still praying that the bell would ring and let me off, but no such luck.

"Peaches?" said Mrs Bradbeer with a kindly smile.

I dragged myself to my feet.

"Peaches McBride," I said. Well, I mumbled it actually, hoping that maybe people wouldn't hear. Stupid, really.

They were obviously going to find out what my surname was as soon as the register was taken, though maybe if it was just read out along with a whole load of other names, no one would notice. No one would put two and two together and go, "Hey! That's the name of that radio person's daughter." Cos Dad *is* quite well known, and just last year they'd done a thing about him in one of the newspapers. An article, with photographs. I'd done my best to hide behind Coop, but you could still see that I had blonde hair.

Fortunately it didn't seem likely that anyone would have read the article, because after all, why should they? Probably none of them ever listened to the radio. It might be like some kind of god in my house, but I bet to most people it is ancient technology. And even if they did listen, they wouldn't be listening to Dad. He is not at all cool.

Zoe, on the far side of the room, called across to me. "Speak louder!"

"Cheek," muttered Millie.

Mrs Bradbeer nodded at me encouragingly. "Just a little bit more volume?"

For a moment I had wild thoughts of claiming to be an orphan, but that was a bit too mad even for me, so instead I gabbled really fast.

"I live with my mum and dad plus two brothers and two sisters with me being in the middle. We used to have some stick insects but they died and we never got any more. I have only one big ambition and that is to concentrate on just being me." And then I said, "Thank you," and sat down.

"Thank *you*," said Mrs Bradbeer.

I could feel my cheeks pulsating. Zoe sniggered, and so did one or two others. I don't think they'd have done it if she hadn't. It was like they all followed her.

"That was OK," whispered Millie.

I smiled weakly. I didn't think it was OK. I thought it was just *stupid*. What had I gone and said thank you for? What was that all about?

There was only one person left, a girl called Janine

who looked like a garden gnome. She was tiny and stubby with a completely round face like an apple and little black buttons for eyes. She bounced up as if she were on springs. She said, "I'm Mouse," and everybody laughed. Well, everybody that had been at Juniors. Mouse was obviously popular. I wondered if I would ever be, but I thought probably not. You can't really be popular if you are anonymous.

As Mouse finished telling us about herself – one brother, two cats, and her dad was a dentist – the bell rang, which meant we had to move on to our next lesson. I took out my timetable. Science, with Miss Jackman. As we left the classroom, Millie said, "Can I ask you something?"

I said, "Of course," and at once became all tensed up, waiting for her to say, "Your dad isn't that man on the radio, is he?"

"I don't mean to be rude," said Millie, "but who are you when you're not being you?"

I was relieved she hadn't asked about Dad, but didn't

quite understand what she meant. She was looking at me expectantly, her head cocked to one side. She had this very vivid face, all scrunched up and eager, with bright eyes that sparkled wickedly.

"You said you wanted to concentrate on being you?"

"Oh! Yes." I was embarrassed. Of all the pathetic things to say! It had just slipped out, probably as a result of nerves. Shamefaced, I said, "It's just sometimes I can't quite decide who I really am?"

If that made any sense, which it almost certainly didn't. This was not a good start! I'd only been at the school for about three hours and already I'd made a complete idiot of myself.

"What I mean," I said lamely, "is it's like I'm one person in my head and another person when I'm, like, *with* people, sort of thing."

Like that made it any better. Probably just made me sound like a total lunatic. But Millie was nodding enthusiastically.

"Same here! It's like sometimes when you hear

yourself talking and you think, is this really me saying all that stuff? Or is this other one really me? This one that's sitting back listening? And then you think, who is the *real* me? Who is the real anybody? How are you supposed to know?"

I thought that some people seemed to know OK. I couldn't imagine any of my family stopping to ask themselves who they were.

"Sometimes," I said, "I can't make up my mind whether I'm just Peachy or whether there's something more."

Millie skipped out of the way as two huge Year 10s went lumbering past.

"Why *just* Peachy?" she said.

I've always been Just Peachy. Almost ever since I can remember.

"It's what my family call me," I said. "Well, it's not what they actually *call* me. It's not like a nickname or anything. It's more what they say, like, 'Oh, it's just Peachy.' Like there was this one time, when I was little, we'd gone to visit my gran…" Big Gran, it was. "I was clambering round the room on the furniture and I went and fell off and clonked my head and started howling, and Gran came rushing in wanting to know what had happened, and Mum said, 'It's all right, you don't have to worry, it's just Peachy.'"

"What did she say that for?" said Millie. "It seems a bit mean."

"I suppose – " I wanted to be fair to Mum, even though it was Gran who had picked me up and cuddled me – "I suppose cos I was the sort of child that was always doing that sort of thing."

"Even so," said Millie. And then she screwed up her face and said, "Families!"

I wondered what hers was like, with all those annoying little sisters. The twins were a bit annoying, always showing off and doing their special twin thing, like finishing each other's sentences or collapsing into secretive peals of laughter. They would giggle away for minutes on end, without anyone ever knowing why.

"Know what?" said Millie. "I was having this huge big argument with my dad the other day and he was getting really mad. I could see him getting all bright red. And in the end he said, 'You have absolutely no idea what you're talking about. You are a mere child.'"

"Like that means you're not entitled to have opinions?" I said.

"I guess not," said Millie. "Not according to my dad."

"Honestly," I said. "Families!"

The second bell was ringing as we reached the science lab. We had been dawdling rather; all the others had raced ahead. Guiltily we made our way down to the front, to the last two empty places. Miss Jackman stood watching us, starched and crackly in her white coat.

"Just get a move on, you two! You should have been here five minutes ago."

You two. I liked that! I think Millie did too, cos she gave another of her impish grins as we slid on to our stools. Seconds later, she pushed a scribbled note along the bench:

"Hi, Just Peachy! This is your friend Merely Millie. LOL!"

I think that was the moment when I began to feel that maybe Sacred Heart would not be so bad. When Gran asked me if I had made any friends yet, I was able to tell her very proudly that I had.

"Excellent," said Gran. "I'm sure that must be a great relief to your mum. I know she was a bit worried."

Mum has this belief that I am shy. But I really am not! So long as I can just be *me*. The reason I'd found it so difficult to make friends at primary school was because of everyone always expecting me to be someone else. All the really cool kids lost interest once they discovered I wasn't like Charlie. And all the others were too busy trying to get into the smart set to bother with a non-entity who'd been dismissed as boring. That only left a few nerdy ones, which made me think I must be pretty nerdy myself, only how can you tell? I wasn't nerdy like Ginetta Derby, who used to keep whining at me to get autographs for her. It was all she was interested in: autographs.

"Your dad must know hundreds of stars! He must meet them all the time. *Please*, Peachy… I really need him to get some for me!"

And then there was Emily Ashton, who trailed round with me at break time and did nothing but moan.

"Everyone is so mean! They are all so *mean*. I really hate them!"

And poor Jennifer Baxter, who couldn't help being nerdy cos her nose kept dripping and whenever you sat next to her all you could hear was the sound of snuffling and sniffing. It absolutely wasn't her fault and I felt really sorry for her and tried very hard not to mind. It wasn't actually the sniffing that bothered me so much as the fact that she was a bit limp and dim, though I expect that was something else she couldn't help.

In the end we all became friends, sort of. We used

to hang out together, the other three nerds and me. Ginetta, whining for autographs, Emily hating everyone, Jennifer sniffing, and me wishing I could be someone else. Someone who *didn't* have a dad that was a minor celeb and brothers and sisters that were so talented and so popular.

And now, at last, I was! That is, I could pretend that I was, and no one would know any different. As far as Millie was concerned I was just me. If she called me Just Peachy, which she sometimes did, it was done as a joke. Just Peachy and Merely Millie!

Gran wanted to know if I was in a group.

I said, "Group?"

"Yes," said Gran, "we used to go round in groups. Well, we called them gangs in those days, but I don't suppose you're allowed to do that now. What with the riots and everything."

Sometimes I find it difficult to follow Gran's train of thought.

"All the violence," said Gran. "Drugs. Guns. *Knives*."

"Oh," I said. "I don't think we have any of that."

"I should hope not!" said Gran. "Not at Sacred Heart. I just wondered if you were part of a group, or—"

"No," I said. "It's just me and this other girl."

"Your own special friend! Your mum must be so pleased."

Mum didn't even know. She'd asked me once or twice, rather vaguely, if I was getting on all right, and I'd said that I was, but I hadn't yet got around to telling her about Millie. I was going to have to soon, cos Millie had suggested only the other day that maybe I could go round to her place one weekend for a sleepover.

"It'd be fun," she said, "wouldn't it?"

I'd agreed that it would. I'd never been to a sleepover before. Me and the nerds hadn't done things like that. There was only one big problem, and that was how I was going to explain to Millie that I couldn't invite her back. Because I couldn't! I really couldn't. I *so* didn't want her discovering about my family.

"Peaches?" said Gran.

"Yes," I said. "Sorry!"

"Would you like to put your mum back on the phone?"

I went into the hall and yelled up the stairs, *"Mu-u-um*! D'you want to speak to Gran again?"

"Love to!" cried Mum. "Oops, watch out!"

I stood stolidly at the foot of the stairs as Mum laughingly slid down the banister. It is not really what you expect from someone of her age, but she likes to show that she can still do it. She can do handstands too, and almost the splits. I suppose it is a good thing.

"Well, you had a nice long chat," she said, landing cat-like at my feet.

I said, "Yes," and handed her the phone. Nobly I resisted the temptation to park myself by the door and listen, though I knew that they would talk about me. Gran would say how good it was that I had made a friend, and Mum would go, "Really? She hasn't said anything to me! Why is that girl so secretive?"

And then when she got off the phone she would

ask me. She would want know when I was going to invite Millie over. Mum is hugely sociable. She is always urging us to bring our friends back.

"You must ask her to come for tea!"

What excuse could I possibly make?

CHAPTER FOUR

As it happened, Mum didn't ask me about Millie cos while she was still talking to Gran there was a loud shriek and Charlie came belting down the stairs in one of her panics.

"Mum, Mum, I've lost my new top! I can't find it anywhere, I've looked all over! Mum, you've got to help me, I really need it, I'm going out in five minutes!"

Mum jumped to attention like she always does. She said goodbye to Gran – "Got to go, sudden crisis!" – and went racing off to search for the missing top. (Which was probably just where it was supposed to be: Charlie never bothers to look properly.) While she was upstairs, the twins had a crisis of their own. I could hear them yelling "Mu-u-u-m!" at the tops of their voices. It sounded like they were up in the attics. I heard Mum call, "All right, I'm coming!" And then the sound of her feet pounding up the attic stairs. No sooner had she got the twins sorted than Dad came roaring in, bellowing like some large jungle creature.

"Cretinous load of pillocks!"

Someone had obviously upset him. People are always upsetting Dad. According to him, the world is full of morons. Mum had to pour him a drink and calm him down, and by that time she'd obviously forgotten about me having a new friend and how lovely it was. At any rate, she didn't return to the subject. But next morning at school Millie mentioned again about us having a sleepover.

"Could you come this Friday? It would be so fun!"

I promised that I would ask Mum that same evening.

"Oh, do," begged Millie. "Please!"

"I will," I said. "I will!"

It's next to impossible, in our house, pinning Mum down for more than a couple of seconds. You have to make a real effort. I knew it wasn't any good trying to do it while the others were around, so I waited till she went upstairs and managed to corner her as she came out of the bathroom. She said, "For goodness sake, Peachy, what are you lurking there for? I nearly tripped over you!"

I didn't waste any time. I said straight out, "Is it OK on Friday if I go to a sleepover?"

"A sleepover?" Mum seemed surprised and pleased. *Peachy? Going to a sleepover?* "Darling, how lovely! Of course it is."

"Thank you," I said.

Hooray! So that was it. I was about to go galloping off when Mum seemed to remember that there were things she was supposed to check. She wasn't used to me going to sleepovers. Or anywhere at all really. Me and the nerds hadn't ever seen one another out of school.

"Whose sleepover is it, exactly?"

"Just a friend," I said. "A girl in my class."

"Oh, yes, your gran said you'd made a friend. Who is she? What's she called?"

"Millie," I said.

"Millie. That's a nice name! Where does she live?"

I hesitated. "Over Marketside?"

"Marketside?" I could see a slight ripple of doubt pass across Mum's face. She is not at all a snob, but Marketside is this area that has a really rough reputation. It was one of the places where there had been riots, with buildings being set on fire and policemen having bottles thrown at them. Even I had been a bit taken aback when Millie said that was where she lived. She'd looked at me challengingly as she said it, though all I'd thought, to be honest, was that it must be a bit scary.

"Millie's a high-flyer," I said. I knew Mum would like that. "She got a scholarship."

"Clever girl," said Mum.

"She is," I said. "Some of the others are a bit sniffy, cos, you know, they look down on people that have got scholarships?"

I wanted to make sure that Mum wasn't one of them, but she said at once that that was ridiculous. "If anything, they ought to look *up*."

Eagerly I said, "That's what I think."

As I was leaving for school on Friday morning, with my nightie and my toothbrush packed away in my school bag, Mum asked me what time I thought I'd be coming back.

"Some time in the afternoon?" I wasn't sure about the rules for sleepovers.

"Well, give me a ring," said Mum. "I'll come and pick you up."

"You don't have to," I said. "I won't be late."

"Don't be silly," said Mum. "Of course I'll come."

"But I can get the bus! Millie's dad," I told her, "is a bus driver."

"So you think he's going to get his bus out just to drive you back?"

"No, I meant—" What had I meant? I hadn't meant anything. Except maybe to impress upon Mum that Millie's dad was a perfectly respectable person even if he did live in a place where people threw bottles and set fire to buildings.

Mum just laughed and told me again not to be silly.

"I'll wait for you to call."

At the end of school me and Millie went to the bus stop to catch a bus to Marketside. I felt quite adventurous. Not only was I going to my first sleepover, I was going there *on a bus*. I'd hardly ever been on a bus. Either Mum or Dad, usually Mum, always drove us everywhere. Mum is not overprotective, but buses just don't figure in her scheme of things. It is either the car, or a cab. There is a family joke that Dad once got on a bus and said to the driver, "42 Tay Hill, please." He thought they actually dropped people off on their doorstep! Well, I don't suppose he really did, but just the idea of Dad getting on a bus cracked everybody up.

I didn't tell any of this to Millie. She was already surprised that I didn't have a bus pass and didn't even know how to get a ticket from the ticket machines.

"Your mum still drives you to school?" she said. She sounded almost accusing.

Quickly I told her that it was only because Mum had to drive the others and could drop me off on the way.

"I s'pose really I could use the bus."

"It would be a lot greener," said Millie.

And in any case it is good to be independent. Millie wanted to know where I lived, so she could tell me which bus to take. When I said, "Tay Hill," she widened her eyes and said, "Ooh, posh!"

"Not really," I said. "We're not! I mean, *some* people are—"

"Like that MP man," said Millie. "I read about him in the paper."

The MP man lived just a few houses up the road from us. Dad sometimes played golf with him.

"Snotgrass," said Millie. "Or whatever his name is."

"Snodgrass." I giggled. Dad said he was a buffoon, even if they did play golf together.

A number 10 bus came and we got on, me clutching my newly purchased ticket.

"Is this the bus your dad drives?" I said.

Millie said, "No, Dad's the 234. He goes all the way to London."

She sounded really proud. I thought that driving a bus in and out of London was probably a lot more important than just driving locally. Like driving a long-distance lorry was more important than driving a little local truck. What Mum would call the *crème de la crème*.

"The cream of the cream," I said.

"You what?" said Millie.

"Your dad! Driving all the way to London every day."

Millie grinned. "I'll tell him."

"Oh, no, please," I begged. "Don't!"

"Why not? He'd like it. *My friend Peachy says you're the cream of the cream.* Oh, look!" She pointed out of the window. "That's where I used to go to school. See? St Jude's Primary. It's where *they* go – the Diddy People."

She meant her little sisters.

"Over *there* – " she pointed straight ahead – "is where the riots were. They burned a whole row of shops. I could see the flames from my bedroom window. And this one boy that lives in our street? He was done for nicking stuff. Police found loads of television sets in his house. Stupid or what?"

I couldn't think of anything to say. I hadn't even known the riots were happening till I heard about it on the news next morning. Millie had been there in the thick of it.

"Went on all night," she said. "Gangs of people walking up and down the street. All going to join in, like going to a party. Then a bit later on you'd see them come back, carrying stuff."

I nodded knowingly. "Stuff they'd nicked."

"Crazy stuff. I mean, just anything they could lay their hands on. Like they'd see a shop smashed open and they'd go rushing in and grab whatever was there. Like cans of lager, for instance. Who'd risk going to prison for nicking cans of lager?"

I shook my head. I wouldn't run the risk of going to prison for nicking anything. I'm not brave enough! Not to mention the fact that stealing is wrong, unless maybe your children are starving and you don't have any money. That, I think, would be understandable, though Dad would not agree with me. Dad is very hard line. He says there is never any excuse for antisocial behaviour.

"Some of them," said Millie, "were only kids. Like our age, roaming the streets at two o'clock in the morning. Dad said they let themselves get all whipped up by what was happening. He said most of them weren't really bad."

I didn't tell him what my dad had said. "Horsewhip the lot of 'em if I had my way!"

"I guess it's different if they're setting things alight," I said.

"Oh, well, yes," said Millie. "There isn't any excuse for that." She sprang up. "This is our stop!"

Millie lived in a street just a few minutes away, in the smallest house I'd ever seen. It was in the middle of a whole row of houses, all the same. There weren't any front gardens, and I think they must have been really old as they had chimney stacks tottering up into the sky, though Millie said the chimneys weren't actually used any more.

"They're all blocked off. Couldn't get a fire going even if you wanted to."

I thought that was a shame. It has always seemed to me that a roaring big fire would be far more cosy than central heating. Millie, however, seemed doubtful.

"Not according to my gran. According to her, they were nothing but a load of hard work." She opened the front door with her own key and called up the stairs, "Mum! We're here!"

A voice with an Irish accent called back: "With you in a minute!"

"Come through," said Millie.

We went along this tiny narrow passage and into the kitchen, where three small girls, standing in a row, solemnly stared at us. They all had jet-black hair cut short with a fringe, and the same bright, inquisitive eyes as Millie. They were so alike they could almost have been triplets, except that they were obviously different ages.

"These are the terrible trio," said Millie. "I'd introduce you, but I can never remember which one is which."

"You so can!" they chorused indignantly.

"I so can't!" said Millie.

"So can!"

"So can't! *Ow.*" The three of them had started pummelling her, pounding at her with their fists. It was obviously a game they played. "All right, all right!" Millie backed away. "Let me see. I think this one is... Katy?"

"*That* one!"

"That one? OK! So if she's Katy, you have to be... Kimberley?"

"*She's* Kimberley!"

"She's Kimberley? OK, OK, I'm getting there! That just leaves... Kaylee! Right? Now I can introduce you. This is my friend Peaches."

The oldest girl, Kaylee, gravely held out her hand. Equally gravely, I took it. So then the other two held out their hands, and I had to take them as well.

"Otherwise known," said Millie, "as the Diddy People. *Ow!*"

Millie's mum came into the kitchen at that point. She looked just like an older version of Millie and her sisters.

"Well, now," she said, "isn't that lovely? Only a short time at the school and already you've found a friend. I knew you would! Peaches, is it? Lovely to meet you, Peaches. That's a beautiful name you have. Now, you three, hop along into the other room while we sort out some food for these two. You can take it upstairs, if you like? If you'd rather be private."

Millie said private would be nice. "There's not a lot of it going on in this house," she said, as we went upstairs carrying a tray of food. "Those Diddy People get everywhere."

She said it like she was complaining, but she obviously loved them.

"I think your sisters are really cute," I said.

"They're OK," said Millie. "But does one actually need *three* of them?" And then she remembered and said, "Of course, you've got even more. I don't suppose you have any privacy at *all*."

I said, "Well..." and let my voice sort of trail away. Lack of privacy is not a problem I have ever had to face. Our house is quite big and we all have our own rooms, so it's easy to shut yourself away if that is what you want. But Millie's house was like a dolls' house, and I noticed immediately that there were bunk beds in her room, so I guessed she had to share with one of her sisters.

"Kaylee," she said. She screwed up her face, making her nose go all crinkled. "That's hers, the top one. But it's all right – she's in with the others for tonight. We've got one of those bedroll things." I must have looked blank. So many things I didn't know about! "You roll them out and sleep on them? Be nice if she always slept there, but there's not really enough space."

There wasn't any space in Millie's room, even without a bedroll thing. We sat companionably on the floor, on a woolly rug, to eat our tea.

"How d'you manage about homework?" I said. We get quite a lot of it at Sacred Heart. "How d'you concentrate?"

"Front room," said Millie. "Me mam's put a desk in

there, and the computer. Nobody's let in till I've finished. Me mam – oops!" She stopped, and clapped a hand to her mouth. "Shouldn't have said that, should I?"

Said what? Me mam? I looked at her, puzzled, as I inserted the straw in my carton of juice. "Why shouldn't you?"

"Not proper use of English. Sister Agatha told me off about it."

"Oh," I said. "Sister Agatha." She was one of the strictest of the nuns. She took us for English and made us all quiver and quake. The only other nun who actually took classes, Sister Marie Clare, who took us for music, was really sweet and gentle. We loved Sister Marie Clare. She would never have told Millie off for saying "me mam".

"My *muthah*," said Millie, sounding like the Queen. "*Thet* is the way one should speak."

I giggled. "What were you going to say about your *muthah*?"

"Oh, just that she reckons if I've been lucky enough

to be given a scholarship I've got to really work hard and show that I deserve it. She was the one that pushed me into it. Her and Mrs Hennessy at primary school. I didn't want to! I wanted to go to Winterbourne with all me friends. *My* friends," she corrected herself.

"I wanted to go to Winterbourne," I said.

"Really? Why didn't you?"

"Mum thought it was too big and I'd get lost."

"How about the others? Where do they go?"

"Well, the twins are still at primary. Coop and Charlie—" I sucked vigorously on my straw. "They're at this place where my dad used to go."

"Is it posh?"

I said no, though in fact it is, quite. It's where the MP sends his son.

"So why didn't you go there?" said Millie.

I tried to think of a reason. "It's got boys," I said. "I have enough of boys at home."

"I have enough of girls," said Millie. "Not that I'm

boy crazy or anything. I think it's pathetic when girls can think of nothing except boyfriends. I mean, *yuck*! But you want to try living with three Diddy People."

I thought that I wouldn't mind if they were as sweet as Millie's little sisters.

"They are just so cute," I said. "And it's amazing, how they all look so alike – they could almost be triplets. And if you were photographed with them," I said, "you could even be…" I couldn't think of the word. "What's it called when people have four babies all at once?"

"Quadruplets." Millie did the thing with her nose, making it go all crinkled. "How about your lot? Do you all look the same?"

I shook my head as I sucked again at my straw, glugging up the last few drops from the bottom of the carton. I don't look like *anyone* in my family. Charlie and Coop are quite big, like Dad, with dark hair. The twins are smaller, and more gingery, like Mum, with pale skin and freckles. I am a *bit* big, which is to say I am not small, and I do have pale skin, but my hair is blonde and I'm the only one with blue eyes, so that nobody ever says, "Oh! Aren't you like your dad?" or, "Ooh, you take after your mum!" like they do with the others.

When I was little I used to have this fantasy that I'd been kidnapped from royalty and then abandoned, and that Mum and Dad had found me in an orphanage. I think I must have read a story where this had happened. When I got a bit older I stopped thinking that I was royalty but still felt that I had to be *someone* – someone different, that is. I even (eek!) used to wonder if Mum had had a secret love affair and that Dad wasn't my real dad at all. But they are so much in love that I don't honestly think this can have been the case. I am just odd, and that is all there is to it.

Millie was looking at me expectantly.

"So what are they like?" she said. "Your lot?"

"Mm... well." I busied myself unwrapping a Kit Kat. "They're OK. I'm sort of... in the middle."

"Better than being the oldest. At least you don't have to act as babysitter. Or do you?"

"No," I said. "I don't have to do that."

I nibbled on my Kit Kat. Millie sat waiting. I had to tell her something, it was only fair. It's what friends do: they ask about each other's families. I'd heard all about hers, about her mum being a school dinner lady and her dad driving his bus all the way up to town. Now it was my turn.

"You don't have to tell me if you don't want," said Millie. "I expect I'm just being nosy."

But she wasn't. She was just taking a normal interest. With fierce concentration I started folding my Kit Kat wrapper into a concertina as I told her about Charlie having played Gwendolen in a musical version of *The Importance of Being Earnest* and how it was Coop that had written the music.

Millie said, "Wow!" Her eyes widened. "He wrote the *music*?"

"It's what he does," I said. "He's like some kind of musical prodigy."

"Like Mozart!"

"Dunno about that," I said.

Sister Marie Claire was into Mozart. She was always playing us bits in the hope that some of it would rub off on to us and stop us listening to nothing but pop, but to me it just sounded tinkly. Not a bit like the sort of stuff that Coop wrote.

"He did this thing called *Holes*," I said. "All crashing and banging. The reason it's called *Holes* is cos every few bars there's, like, total silence? Like a row of knitting with dropped stitches."

Actually, as far as I was concerned, the silences came as a relief cos the music itself was just noise. Well, that was how it seemed to me. It didn't have any tune. It didn't have any rhythm. You couldn't sing to it; you couldn't dance to it. But I'm not musical, so what do

I know? Mum says he's a genius, and she is probably right.

"You ought to tell Sister Marie Clare," said Millie. "She'd be well impressed!"

I wriggled uncomfortably. "That'd be like boasting."

"It wouldn't if I told her."

I bent my head over my concertina, carefully folding it in half, and then half again, only second time round it was too thick and wouldn't fold properly. Millie sat watching me. I looked up and saw that she was frowning.

"I won't tell her if you'd rather I didn't," she said. "Not if it's supposed to be a secret."

I said that it wasn't a secret, it was just...

"What?"

"Just..."

"It's all right." Millie said it kindly, like she'd taken pity on me. "'Tisn't any of my business. Let's get this stuff downstairs and I'll show you where I do my homework."

I'd often wondered what actually happened when

you went to a sleepover. I had this vague idea that you might try out new hairstyles, or make-up, or play games on the computer. Then later, when it was dark and you were safely tucked up in bed, you'd tell each other ghost stories and make your flesh creep. Oh, and eat stuff! Popcorn, or sardines, or toasted marshmallows. Not that I actually knew what toasted marshmallows were; I think they were just something I'd read about in books. Most of my ideas seemed to come from books. Real life often turned out to be quite different.

Like my sleepover with Millie. We didn't do any of the stuff I thought we'd do. Neither of us was really very interested in hairstyles or make-up, and playing games on the computer would have meant staying downstairs in the front room, which wasn't anywhere near as cosy as Millie's bedroom. We did try a few ghost stories, but we weren't very good at it and Millie got the giggles, which gave me the giggles, and her mum came into the room and said, "Girls, it's one o'clock in the morning!"

Millie said, "Sorry, sorry, we'll be quiet as mice."

"You could maybe try going to sleep," said her mum; but we were far too wide awake for that.

We'd spent the whole evening talking. Just talking! We'd talked about school, about our favourite subjects and our favourite teachers. We'd talked about our favourite books, our favourite TV programmes, our favourite singers. I'd never met anyone I felt so at home with as I did with Millie. I reckoned we could have gone on talking all night without ever running out of subjects.

We almost did go on all night. Every now and then there'd be a bit of a silence, then one of us would go, "Are you asleep?" and the other one would bounce over in her bunk and go, "No! Are you?" and that would set us off again.

Next morning I met Millie's dad. He was a little tubby man with sandy hair and a bald patch in the middle and I was terrified in case Millie did what she had threatened to do and told him how I'd said he was the cream of the cream. She'd obviously remembered cos she gave me this impish grin like, *Shall I tell?* and I felt my cheeks grow all hot and hectic. Katy, the smallest of the Diddy People, immediately squealed, "Peachy's gone pink!" And then she gave a reproachful yelp as Millie kicked her under the table. I know it was Millie cos she told me so later. She said, "No manners, the younger generation." And then she added, "You needn't have worried — I wasn't going to say anything."

I was grateful to her. It would have been too embarrassing!

"I knew you didn't want me to," said Millie, "so that's why I wasn't going to. Friends have got to be able to trust each other."

When it came time to go home, later that afternoon, Millie's mum wanted to know whether anyone was coming to pick me up or would I like a lift?

"She wants to go by bus," said Millie. "I'm going to take her down the bus stop and make sure she gets the right one."

Millie fussed over me like a mother hen. She said, "Get *off* the bus at the Town Hall Gardens, stay *right where you are* and wait for the number 2b." She repeated it. "2b. Yes?"

"Yes." I nodded.

"That'll take you to the bottom of Tay Hill. Then when you come to school on Monday you can get the same bus all the way. Dead easy!"

I felt quite proud of myself, buying my ticket, getting on and off buses all on my own. Pathetic, really, but everyone has to start somewhere. Mum was surprised when I walked in.

"I thought you were going to call me?" she said.

Carelessly I told her that I had come by bus. "It's dead easy! And a whole lot greener than cluttering up the roads with private cars."

Mum said, "Be as green as you like, but just don't use that word in front of your dad."

Dad is one of those people that thinks global warming is a government plot. It is something that makes him very angry. But then there are just so many things that make Dad angry.

"Anyway, I take it you enjoyed yourself?" said Mum.

I assured her that I had.

"Well, don't forget," said Mum, "next time it'll be Millie's turn to come here."

CHAPTER FIVE

"Omigod, that was awesome!" said Millie, on Monday morning. "Dad said we're like a pair of old gossips. Yack, yack, yack! He said he couldn't think what we found to talk about all that time. I told him," said Millie, "we could have gone on talking all night." She slipped her arm through mine. "We must do it again!"

I knew she was waiting for me to say, "Yes, and next time you must come round to mine."

If only Mum and Dad and all the others would just go away somewhere for the weekend and leave me on my own. But some hopes! Mum wouldn't hear of it.

"You do *want* to do it again?" Millie sounded anxious. "Say if you don't! I won't be hurt."

But she would be; anyone would be. And I *did* want to! I just didn't want Millie finding out about Dad and having to be introduced to the rest of the family. I didn't think I could bear it if Millie got all blown away by Coop and Charlie, same as everyone else. I could still remember a girl in my class at Juniors going, "Charlie McBride is your *sister?*" Like on the one hand, *Wow!* and on the other hand, *You've got to be joking!* With her eyes swivelling all over me and this look of pitying wonderment on her face. How could the great Charlie McBride have a sister like that?

I so didn't want the same sort of look from Millie!

I assured her that I couldn't wait for us to have

another sleepover. "And this time we *will* talk all night!"

"Let's do it really soon," begged Millie.

I said that I would ask Mum. But I kept putting it off and putting it off, so that when Millie reminded me, a few days later, I had to quickly think up an excuse, like I hadn't had a chance, Mum had been just *so* busy.

"She's always, like, flying around, you know?"

"You mean like properly flying?" said Millie.

Idiotically I said yes. Stupid, stupid, *stupid*. Mum hates flying! She is always scared that the plane is going to plummet.

"I *will* ask her," I said. "Soon as I can get hold of her."

Millie didn't remind me again, she probably thought it would be too much like nagging, but I knew she was eagerly waiting for me to come up with something.

Mum had said, "Don't forget," and I didn't, cos how could I? It nagged at me all the time. I felt sure that sooner or later Mum was bound to ask me, "When are you having Millie over for that sleepover?" But then, before she could do so, things happened that put me and Millie right out of her mind. Things are always happening in the McBride house. There is never a dull moment.

First off, Dad was shortlisted for yet another radio award, and we all went out to celebrate. Dad kept saying, "Whoa! Just because I've been shortlisted doesn't mean I'm necessarily going to win." But we all knew it probably did. Dad is hugely popular, though I'm not quite sure why. I guess listeners enjoy it when he's rude to people and shouts over the top of them and says that their views are moronic.

Anyway, no sooner had we gone out celebrating with Dad than the twins took part in some horsey thing, a gymkhana, and we all had to go and cheer them on as they jumped their tiny little ponies over enormous great jumps and had them weaving in and out of poles and doing other clever things, for which they both won rosettes. A woman came up to Mum and barked, "Amazing kids! Brilliant little riders. Wouldn't be surprised if we see them representing England one of these days."

Mum beamed and said, "The next Olympics!"

Two days later Charlie came bubbling home with the news that she had been picked for the school's hockey team.

"The *first* team, Mum! I'm the youngest player they've ever had!"

So that was another celebration. We do a LOT of celebrating in our family. At least it made Mum forget about Millie coming for a sleepover, so I was grateful for that though of course it didn't solve my problem. I knew I couldn't go on putting Millie off for ever.

And then I had an idea. Suppose I invited Millie back, like the following weekend, but then at the last minute I told her my gran had rung and was paying us a visit: "It means I'll have to move in with Flora so that Gran can have my room!"

Millie would be almost certain to suggest that I went back to her place again instead. Wouldn't she?

Yesss!

I was all set to put my plan into action when Gran herself went and ruined it. She actually did ring up! Not to say that she was coming to visit, but she must have asked after me or done something to jog Mum's memory, cos immediately she put the phone down Mum turned to me, quite accusingly, and said, "I thought you were going to ask Minnie to stay over?"

"Millie," I said.

"Millie. Yes! So when are you going to do it? How about this Friday?"

I couldn't see any way out. Well, I suppose I could have told Mum that Millie was doing something else on Friday, but I couldn't *keep* telling her that. Sooner or later she would start to get suspicious and think we'd fallen out. Then she would discuss it with Gran – "Something's gone wrong, I think they must have quarrelled." Then Gran would want to talk to me and find out what had happened. Worst of all, Millie might decide she didn't want me as a friend any more. I did *so* wish I had a normal family! An ordinary family. Like Millie's. A mum that was a school dinner lady, a dad that drove buses. And three funny little Diddy People!

But you get what you are given. You can't choose what you are born into. And in any case, as I reminded myself, not everyone sees things the same way. Maybe Millie would meet my family and think they *were* just ordinary.

I could only hope.

She was so happy when I asked her. Her whole face lit up. She said, "Ooh, yes please, I'd love to!"

I at once decided that I would stop being what Dad calls a worry wart, always imagining the worst and thinking up disasters. Me and Millie were going to have fun! With any luck Charlie would be out with her latest boyfriend (she went through boys at the rate of about one a week) and Dad would be at one of his special fundraising dinners. They were the two I most didn't want Millie to meet. I wasn't so bothered about Coop.

He is not as intimidating as Charlie and when he is in the throes of one of his compositions he tends to live in a world of his own. He probably wouldn't even notice that I had Millie round. As for the twins, they are just something that has to be put up with. Like hurricanes or a force-ten gale.

I asked Mum, "On Friday, when Millie comes over, can we take our tea straight up to my room?"

"If that's what you want," said Mum. "So long as you at least stop off to say hello before disappearing."

I said, "Absolutely!" Thinking to myself that all we had to do was say hello to Mum, then scuttle upstairs as fast as could be and shut ourselves away.

Friday after school we walked down to the bus stop together. Proudly I told Millie that I always got the bus now.

"It's much better than Mum driving me," I said.

"I'll tell my dad," said Millie. "I'll tell him I've converted you!"

When we got off the bus at the bottom of Tay Hill,

Millie stopped her usual chattering and fell strangely silent. She kept glancing about her at the houses and seemed uncomfortable.

"Which one is yours?" she said.

I pointed. "That one over there."

"I thought you said it wasn't posh!"

"It's not," I said, but looking at it through Millie's eyes I could see that it might appear so. "Honestly," I said, "it's just got lots of rooms."

"Lots of rooms *is* posh," muttered Millie.

"Not really," I said. "Last year the roof sprung a leak and we had to keep running up and down to the attics with buckets!"

"You've got *attics?*" said Millie.

We've got a basement as well, but I didn't tell her that. I hoped she wouldn't notice.

Mum was in the kitchen; so were the twins. They were both shouting at the tops of their voices. Something about this very special pony that they simply had to have.

"He's a palomino!"

"He's gorgeous!"

They briefly broke off as me and Millie came in, then immediately started up again.

"Ginny's grown out of him, Mum, that's why they're selling him on."

"We could still keep either Polo or Whisky."

"*Mum?*"

They hovered, like a couple of annoying little tug boats bobbing up and down on a choppy sea.

"Mum, *please?* Can we?"

"I don't know," said Mum. "I can't decide anything right now. Go and speak to your father."

My heart sank. Dad was here? I had been so praying he would be out! I didn't want Millie being frightened. Dad can be really overwhelming.

"Right." Mum shooed the terrible pair, still clamouring, out of the kitchen, and closed the door. "Minnie! How lovely to meet you at last."

"Millie," I said.

"Millie! Of course. So sorry! Terrible with names."

"It's very kind of you to have me," said Millie. I stared at her. Why was she putting on that funny voice, like she was pretending to be the Queen?

"No, no," said Mum. "The pleasure's all mine. I'm just so happy that Peachy's made a friend."

"I understand," said Millie, still in her careful voice, "that you've been doing a lot of flying just lately?"

"Flying?" said Mum. "Me?"

Mum looked puzzled, Millie embarrassed. I jumped in hastily.

"Flying *about*. I was telling Millie how busy you always are."

"Oh. Yes! I suppose I am." Mum said it vaguely, as if she wasn't quite sure. "Help yourself to some tea, whatever you want. There's some…"

The rest of the sentence was drowned out by a piercing shriek of "*Mu-u-u-um!*" as Charlie came bursting through the door. She stopped at the sight of Millie and flapped a hand. "Hi."

Millie said, "Hi," in a rather subdued voice.

"Mum, you've got to help me," begged Charlie. "I can't find my shorts. I need them for the match tomorrow!"

"They're all washed and ironed and put away," said Mum.

"But they're not in my drawer!"

"Of course they're in your drawer. I put them there myself."

Mum disappeared down the hall with Charlie wailing behind her. I said, "That's my sister Charlotte. She's always losing things – she's totally useless. Let's get our tea and go upstairs."

I yanked open the fridge and started grabbing stuff. Cartons of fruit juice, little chocolate pots, carrot sticks. Then I rushed to the cupboard and snatched a couple of bags of crisps and a packet of biscuits. I wanted to get Millie safely smuggled upstairs before the twins or Charlie came crashing back. Unfortunately, on our way down the hall we bumped into Dad barrelling out of the sitting room, shouting as he went.

"Don't badger me! I've told you, I'll think about it!"

He then saw me, with Millie. "Hello!" he said. "Who are you?"

I said, "This is Millie. She's staying the night."

"Really? Jolly good!"

Dad went roaring off, leaving me and Millie to make our way to my bedroom. All along the side of the stairs there are glossy photos of Dad with the awards that he has won. It's Mum who hangs them there; she is very proud of Dad. I am so used to them I almost never notice them any more, but Millie paused, very carefully, to study each one.

"Is your dad famous?" she said.

The smart answer would have been, "If he were famous, you wouldn't have to ask. Ha ha!" But I am not very quick at saying smart things. I only think of them hours afterwards, when it is way too late. So I just wriggled a bit and said, "Not really."

"But he's won all those awards!"

"Only for being on the radio," I said. "It's not like being on the telly."

Millie looked at me doubtfully. "He must be a *bit* famous."

"Just a minor celeb," I said, pulling Millie into my bedroom and firmly shutting the door.

We sat on cushions on the floor to eat our tea. We talked a bit as usual about school, and how some people, such as Zoe Kingman, were rather obnoxious and chucked their weight about – "Thinks she's the big cheese," sniffed Millie – and how others, like Janine Corrie, known as the Mouse, were quite friendly; and Millie told me what the Diddy People were up to, and I told her how the twins were horribly spoilt and always got their own way cos neither Mum nor Dad could bear to say no to them; but it wasn't the same as when we were at Millie's.

It had been so warm and cosy in Millie's cluttered little room. My room was warm, cos of the central heating, but it wasn't *cosy*. There was too much space! Plus I was suddenly aware of how much stuff I had that Millie didn't. My own television, for instance; my laptop. Shelves full of books, and china animals. Big puffy cushions, a walk-in wardrobe full of clothes. I'd always just taken it for granted. Now I had a horrible feeling that it was making Millie uncomfortable.

I was too much of a coward to say anything. Millie is bolder; she always says exactly what is on her mind. As we finished tea she came out with it: "Is this why you didn't want to invite me back?" She waved a hand, taking in my room with all its bits and pieces. "Cos I'm not posh enough?"

I felt my cheeks immediately start to glow. I stammered that of course it wasn't. "And I did want to invite you back!"

"You didn't really," said Millie. She didn't say it accusingly; just stated it like it was a fact. My cheeks by now were sizzling like bacon in a pan.

"Be honest!" she said. "You didn't, did you?"

I swallowed. "It's not like you think."

"It's all right," said Millie. "Dad warned me when I got the scholarship I mightn't find it easy being at a school like Sacred Heart. He didn't really want me to go there; it was Mum who pushed me. Dad said there'd be bound to be some people that were prejudiced. Like Zoe."

"Zoe's just a stupid snob," I said. "Not everyone's like her. *I'm* not like her!"

"You're not when we're at school," said Millie.

"I'm not when I'm at home either!"

Millie looked at me. She was obviously waiting for me to say something.

"If you must know…" I took a breath, trying to stop my voice from wobbling. "If you must know," I gabbled, "the reason I was scared to invite you was cos of Dad."

"Cos of your *dad*?"

"I didn't want you finding out about him!"

Millie giggled. "You make it sound like he's some kind of guilty secret. Like he's been in prison or something!"

Glumly I said, "No. Just on the radio."

"You didn't want me to know he was on the radio?" How pathetic was that? "Why on earth not?" said Millie. "I don't mind you knowing my dad's on the buses."

"That's different."

"You mean, cos my dad's not a celeb?"

"*Minor* celeb."

"Whatever." Millie sat back, cross-legged, on her cushion. "I don't get it!"

I sighed. "It's not just Dad. It's all the rest of the family."

"You saying they're celebs as well? Like your brother writing that bit of music full of holes?"

"Sort of." I hooked my hair behind my ears and tried rather desperately to explain. "I sometimes think it's like living on a film set. You know?" Millie nodded, a bit uncertainly. "Like they're all busy being stars in this huge great movie and I'm stuck in the middle of it trying to be me!"

Millie said, "Ah. Right! Now I'm with you." She nodded. "Just Peachy."

"That's why I asked if I could go to a different school. So's nobody would know who I was."

"Well, that's OK." Millie said it bracingly. "Who's going to find out? Not like your dad's a pop star or anything. And I don't expect," she added, "that people like Zoe are going to listen to a bit of music all full of holes!"

That made me smile a bit, in a watery kind of way.

"She hasn't got the brain for it," said Millie.

I said, "Neither have I. It's all loud and tuneless and horrible."

"Apart from the holes."

I agreed. "The holes are OK. They're quite peaceful."

"Sing me one," said Millie. "How do they go?"

"Like this." I let my mouth fall open.

Millie giggled. "Like this?"

We sat there in solemn silence, our mouths agape, gobbling like goldfish, until in the end we both collapsed.

"Did I stay in tune?" said Millie.

I said, "No! I think you must be tone deaf."

We collapsed all over again.

When we'd recovered Millie said, "So are we all right now? I mean, it doesn't really matter *me* knowing about your dad. Does it?"

I said, "I s'pose not. It's just…" I hesitated, wondering how much I could confess without sounding totally pathetic.

"Just what?" said Millie.

It all came out in a sudden rush, "It's just I didn't want you meeting Charlie!"

"Your sister?" Millie sounded surprised. "The one that's totally useless?"

I said, "Well, she *is* totally useless cos Mum runs round after her all the time, but she's like always being picked for the school play and getting into hockey teams and being asked to loads of parties and having a zillion boyfriends, and I wouldn't mind," I wailed, "except people seem to think I ought to be like her and then they find I'm not and they look at me like I'm just rubbish!"

"Oh, that is so nonsense," said Millie. "We wouldn't be friends if you were rubbish. I don't *make* friends with rubbish people! I only make friends with people I find interesting. People that are funny, and clever. Like you!"

Nobody had ever said that to me before. Funny? And clever?

"You say these funny things," said Millie. "Like about my dad being the cream of the cream. And you *are* clever, cos who got an A for her last bit of homework?"

I'd only got an A cos we had to write about our favourite place in all the world, and I'd written about Cornwall, where I'd once gone on holiday all by myself with Gran. Millie had said that her favourite place was home, and she had got an A*. She was always getting A*.

"Honestly," she said, "I only like clever people.

Otherwise I find them boring. I suppose I shouldn't say that, really. I'm always saying things I shouldn't say. But know what? I don't care! And I don't think you ought to care either. Not about your silly sister *or* your dad. It's like you said at the beginning of term, about concentrating on just being *you*."

"Yes." I nodded humbly. "You're right."

Millie cackled. "I'm always right!" She sprang up and bounced over to my bookshelves. "I've got a game you can play with books. D'you want to try it? What you do, you pick a book and you read bits of it out loud, without saying any of the characters' names, and the other person has to guess what book it is. I invented it," said Millie, "with a friend I had at primary school, only she's at Winterbourne now, so we don't hardly see each other. Anyway, you'll be better at it than she was cos you've got all these books. She practically only read Harry Potter and the Rainbow Fairies. Shall we give it a go?"

I said, "Yes, let's!"

Not being mean or anything, but I was glad Millie wasn't seeing her friend any more. I wanted her to be *my* friend. Just the two of us together.

"I promise," she whispered, as we parted company the next day, "I won't breathe a word about your dad!"

CHAPTER SIX

I got back from school on Monday afternoon to find Charlie in the kitchen with Mum. As soon as I came in she swung round, catching me a hearty thwack on my thigh with her hockey stick. I yelped. "Ow! That hurt!"

"Oh, don't be such a wimp," said Charlie. "Not

like I did it on purpose. Listen, want to hear some news?"

"What?" I said it rather crossly. I wasn't being a wimp! Anyone would object to being whacked by a hockey stick. I wouldn't have minded so much if she'd *apologised*. But she never does. "Look," I said, "it's already coming up in a bruise!"

"Put some arnica on it," said Mum.

"And stop making such a *fuss*. I hardly even touched you!"

"Excuse me," I said, "but being clonked by a hockey stick is really painful."

Charlie made an impatient tutting sound. "Do you want to hear my news or not?"

I didn't particularly, but there is never any stopping her.

"Guess what?" She took a swipe at an imaginary ball and bashed her hockey stick against the leg of the kitchen table. Mum didn't say a word. "We're playing your lot in the next round of the InterSchools

 116 ☆

Hockey tournament!" She announced it with an air of triumph.

Guardedly I said, "Oh?"

"Thursday afternoon," said Charlie. "At your place."

What??? Charlie was coming to Sacred Heart?

"Just make sure you watch!"

"I won't be able to cheer for you," I said.

"Don't expect you to cheer for me. Just expect you to watch."

"I don't know if they'll let us."

"Of course they will!" said Mum. "It's an important event."

"Not as important as lessons," I said quickly. "I don't think Sister Agatha would let us miss a lesson."

"What, not even to watch your own sister?"

Mum sounded indignant. I told her that the nuns were very strict, and that Sister Agatha was the strictest of all.

Mum pulled a face. "I could always write a note, asking her to make an exception."

 117 ☆

"Oh, Mum, no," I begged. "Please!"

"But it's your *sister*," said Mum.

"Yes, but it would seem like favouritism. Please don't!"

Mum looked slightly offended. "Very well, if you insist," she said. "Have it your own way. I was only trying to help."

I prayed that Sister Agatha would be as strict as I'd said she was. Surely she wouldn't consider a hockey match important enough to miss class? Unfortunately, as I belatedly remembered, last period on Thursday was PE, when we normally had to *play* hockey.

"So as a special treat," beamed Sister Agatha, "you may all go and attend the match."

"I wish we could just go home early instead," I said to Millie, thinking that she would be bound to agree with me. Millie isn't any more sporty than I am. "I mean, who wants to have to stand around watching a stupid hockey match?"

"I don't mind *watching*," said Millie. "Just so long as I don't have to join in."

"But it'll be so boring," I moaned. "Maybe we could hide in the library or something."

Millie shook her head. "They'd notice if we weren't there."

"Not if we slipped away really quietly."

"Not worth it," said Millie. "We could get into a whole load of trouble all for nothing."

"Anything's better than having to watch people whacking a ball all up and down."

"Well, it's not what I'd choose," agreed Millie, "but it's not as bad as all that. I'm just happy we're getting out of PE!"

Thursday loomed over me. I kept telling myself that I was simply being silly. Who was going to know that Charlie was my sister? Millie wasn't going to tell anyone. In any case she'd only met her once, for about two seconds; she probably wouldn't even recognise her. I was doing my usual thing, worrying myself sick for no reason.

And then Thursday arrived and I really did get sick.

It happened at the end of the lunch break, as we were about to go back into class. I suddenly came over all limp and sweaty. I thought for a moment that I was going to faint.

"You all right?" said Millie.

I pressed a hand to my mouth. "Think I'm going to throw up."

Millie is not the sort of person to dither.

"Better get you to the sick room," she said; and she took me by the arm and firmly marched me off. I tried bleating a protest, but Millie can be very forceful.

"What's her problem?" said Zoe, passing us in the corridor.

"Going to the sick room," said Millie. "Like it's any of her business," she added under her breath.

I spent the next half-hour lying down, sweating and feeling sick, and then the nurse rang Mum and asked her if she could come and take me home.

"What on earth have you been up to?" said Mum when she arrived.

"Haven't been up to anything," I said. "I just suddenly came over all funny."

Mum seemed at a bit of a loss. We don't get sick in our family; it's like it's not allowed.

"I hope you're not incubating something." Mum looked at me almost accusingly.

"Like what?" I said.

"I don't know! One of those childhood things… mumps or something? Chicken pox? You haven't got a rash, have you?" She peered at me. "Whatever it is, I just hope it's not catching. I don't want all the others going down with it – especially now, when Charlie and Coop have so much on."

"It's all right," I said, "I won't breathe over them. And actually," I said, "I think I'm starting to feel a bit better. It's such a nuisance, cos it means I'll miss the hockey match."

"Yes, that's a shame," said Mum. "Were they going to let you watch it?"

"Instead of doing PE," I said.

"Well…" Mum glanced at me. "Your colour seems to have come back a bit. Do you want to give it a go? I could always come and watch with you."

"No!" I almost yelped it. Why do I *say* these things? Just trying to impress Mum – that's all it was. Trying to assure her that I'd been really looking forward to seeing Charlie cover herself in glory. Which I knew she would, cos she always does. "I think p'raps it would be more sensible if I went home," I said.

"Well, it's up to you," said Mum.

As soon as school let out, Millie rang on her mobile.

"How are you?"

I told her that I was loads better. "I think it must have been food poisoning or something."

"Hmm." Millie seemed doubtful. "Dunno how you'd have got that."

"School dinner?" I said darkly.

"But we both had the same!"

"I had a pot of yoghurt," I reminded her.

"Don't think yoghurt gives you food poisoning."

"Well, whatever it was," I said, "I'm OK again."

"At least it got you out of having to watch the hockey."

"Was it boring?" I said. I was still hoping she wouldn't have recognised Charlie, all mixed up with a bunch of others. "Did we win?"

"You must be joking! They did... 11–3."

"Does that mean we're out of the tournament?"

"I guess."

I said, "Oh, well."

"Know what?" Millie giggled. "Sister Agatha was there. She actually called out, 'Come on, Sacred Heart!' and started jumping up and down. Can you imagine? Sister *Agatha*?"

I said that I couldn't.

"Honestly, you should have seen her," said Millie. "It was really funny; everyone was giggling."

"I shouldn't have eaten that yoghurt," I moaned. "I knew it didn't taste right."

Millie grunted.

"I'm over it now though," I said.

"Good," said Millie. There was the slightest of pauses, then abruptly she said, "Why didn't you tell me that was the school your sister goes to?"

"I…" I swallowed. "I'd forgotten."

"That she was at Summerfield?"

"That she was in the team."

"She scored five goals," said Millie.

"I know," I said. "She's a genius."

"Dunno about that. Just good at hockey."

"She's good at everything."

Millie's voice came briskly over the phone line. "Nobody's good at everything. That's just silly. Here's my bus, I'm getting on it… I'm on my way up the stairs… see you tomorrow."

I was left with this uncomfortable feeling that Millie hadn't been very sympathetic. She had sounded almost impatient, like it was my own fault I'd been sick. Like Charlie, when she arrived home all flushed with success and eager to know what I thought of the match.

"Who won?" said Mum.

"We did, 11–3, and I scored five goals!"

"Oh, darling, that's wonderful," said Mum. "Wait till your dad hears!"

"Did you watch?" Charlie spun round to look at me. "Did you see that last goal? *Wham!*" She made whacking motions with an imaginary hockey stick. "I couldn't believe it when it went in!"

"Unfortunately," said Mum, "Peachy missed it all. She was feeling sick and I had to go and bring her home."

"You're joking! You didn't see *any* of it? Honestly," grumbled Charlie, "it's almost unbelievable... one of the most important games I've ever played in and she goes and misses it!"

"I'm sorry," I said. "I couldn't help it."

Charlie said, "Huh!" And then, "Trust you."

What did she mean, trust me? It wasn't like I made a habit of getting sick.

"I reckon it was food poisoning," I said.

"Yeah, yeah, yeah!" Charlie grabbed a carton of juice

from the fridge. "I don't think you ever really *wanted* to watch."

"I did!" I said, but it was a feeble kind of protest.

When Dad came in and heard the news he shouted, "That calls for a celebration!" and marched us all up the road to the Indian restaurant. Charlie said, "I'm not sure people with food poisoning ought to be eating curry."

"Food poisoning?" said Dad. "Who's got food poisoning?"

"Oh, just Peachy," said Charlie. "She didn't see *any* of my goals."

Next morning as I got off the bus I heard a voice calling after me: "Hey! Peaches!" I turned and saw Zoe, with a couple of her mates, Rhiannon and Lola. Zoe was waving at me. I slowed down, waiting for her, wondering what she wanted. Zoe and her lot didn't usually take much notice of people like me and Millie.

"Wanted to ask you something," said Zoe. "Is Charlie McBride your sister?"

Without even stopping to think I said, "Who's Charlie McBride?"

"The one that scored half the goals in yesterday's match!"

"And we know she's your sister," said Lola, "cos Millie O'Dowd said she was."

I felt my cheeks go crimson. How could Millie do such a thing? She knew I didn't want people discovering about my family!

"Why is she at Summerfield," said Zoe, "and you're at Sacred Heart?"

"And why say you don't know her?"

They were all looking at me like I was mad.

"Hey!" Lola prodded at me with a bony finger. "Your dad's that man on the radio, right?"

Weakly I said, "What man?"

"That one that's always being rude to people? My mum says he's a shock jock. She says he just likes winding people up so he can yell at them."

"You might have told us," said Zoe.

"Yes, like at the beginning of term, when we all had to introduce ourselves? You didn't say a thing!"

"Didn't want to boast," I mumbled.

"Boast?" Zoe gave a short laugh. "Don't see what's to boast about if he's as rude as all that!"

"Even if he is on the radio," said Lola.

"Right! Might be different if he was on TV."

"He is sometimes," I said, and then immediately wished I hadn't cos they all started jeering.

"Get her!" Zoe pranced triumphantly. "Now she *is* boasting!"

"I'm not," I protested. "I'm just saying."

"Well, you might have said sooner," said Lola. "We all said what *our* dads did."

"Even your friend Millie – *my dad's on the buses*!"

They all sniggered. Normally I would have said something. I would have said that bus drivers did an important and responsible job. Far more important than being rude to people on the radio. But I was still

★ 128 ☆

feeling shaken by Millie's treachery. How *could* she have told them about Charlie?

Millie was already there when I entered our classroom. Her desk was right next to mine. As I sat down she whispered, "You OK now?"

I nodded, but couldn't bring myself to actually say anything.

"You sure?" said Millie. "You look kind of pale."

I frowned, and concentrated on taking my books and pencil case out of my bag.

"Want to hear something funny?" Millie leaned across, giggling. "The ridiculous Diddy People wanted to know when my fruit friend was coming round again. That's what they call you — my fruit friend!"

I pursed my lips.

"Sometimes they pretend they can't remember what sort of fruit you are and they start saying Apple, or Pear, or Strawberry, like they're being *so-o-o* clever!"

I tried to smile but my lips refused to do more than

just quiver. I was relieved when Mrs Bradbeer came in and we all had to stop talking.

At break, me and Millie wandered off together as usual. We'd got into this habit of walking round the edge of the playing field, sharing a Kit Kat or a packet of Maltesers, talking as we went. This morning it was Millie that did all the talking; I stayed silent. After a bit she stopped and said, "What's the matter? Have I done something?"

"You told them about Charlie!" The words came blurting out of me.

Two spots of colour appeared in Millie's cheeks. She said, "I *what?*"

"You told them about Charlie! Even though I begged you not to!"

"Who did I tell?" said Millie.

"Zoe. You told Zoe!"

"Is that what she said?"

"*And* Lola and Rhiannon. They said, 'it was your friend Millie'. And now they know about Dad as well!"

"Oh, boo hoo," said Millie. "So they know about your dad. Big deal!"

"But you *promised*. I trusted you!"

"Strange way to trust someone," said Millie, "going and accusing them."

"I'm not accusing you! I'm just telling you what they said. They said you told them!"

"Know what?" Millie screwed up the Kit Kat wrapper and chucked it in the bushes. It was something she wouldn't normally have done. "You wanna get a grip," she said. "Going all to pieces just because people have found out who your sister is, and who your dad is. Like it's some big dark secret!"

I blinked. I couldn't believe this was Millie talking. Why was she turning on *me*? She was the one in the wrong!

"I mean, look at you," said Millie. "Getting so wound up you even go and make yourself sick! How pathetic is that?"

"I couldn't help it," I said. "It was food poisoning."

"Oh, pur-lease!" Millie rolled her eyes. "What a load of rubbish! You just wanted to run away. Like wanting to come to a different school cos you couldn't take the competition. And then you go and accuse *me*!"

I swallowed, trying to stop the tears welling up in my eyes. "I told you, it was Zoe. If she hadn't said anything, I wouldn't ever have known."

"What, that I'd gone and betrayed you?" The two spots of colour had flared up again in Millie's cheeks. "Some kind of friend you are!"

With that she turned on her heel and went marching back into school, leaving me standing there by myself trying to work out what had happened. Why had she attacked me? What had I done? I hadn't done anything! Just made Millie angry, and I didn't know why. *I* was the one that ought to be angry. But I couldn't be. I was just hurt and bewildered. If Millie had apologised, or said that it was something that had just slipped out by mistake, I could have forgiven her. But she hadn't apologised! And now it was like would she forgive *me*? Even though I wasn't the one that was guilty.

The bell rang, and I trailed miserably back into school. Millie didn't even look at me.

"You two had a row?" said Zoe later.

Had we? I wasn't sure. I just knew that Millie wasn't speaking to me any more.

CHAPTER SEVEN

I was in my bedroom, staring glumly at some maths homework, when the doorbell rang. Almost immediately there was a loud screech of "I'll get it, I'll get it!" followed by the sound of footsteps pounding down the stairs. Charlie. Probably her latest boyfriend.

I returned gloomily to a page of meaningless figures. I don't really get maths. Usually I relied on Millie to help me out, but it seemed like Millie didn't want to be friends any more. She thought I was pathetic.

"*Getting so wound up you even go and make yourself sick!*"

I was still feebly trying to blame it on the yoghurt, though really I had this horrible feeling that Millie might be right. Which could only mean that I was totally mad.

"Hey, Peachy!" Charlie's voice came bellowing up the stairs. "For you!"

Me? I sniffed, in a self-pitying kind of way, and blew my nose, which was feeling a bit soggy. I wasn't *crying*. But I did so hate not being friends with Millie!

Slowly, I shuffled along the landing and peered over the banisters.

"*There* you are," said Charlie. "What took you so long?"

She is always very impatient. Just because she flies about at the speed of light she expects everyone else to do the same. A small figure stepped out from behind her.

"Hi," said Millie.

I said, "H-hi."

"Well, go on," said Charlie. She gave Millie a little shove. "Go up!"

"Don't worry," said Millie, as we went into my room. "I'm not going to yell again. I just came to say that I was sorry."

I swallowed a lump like a hard-boiled egg which seemed to have got stuck in my throat.

Millie pulled a face. "Me Mam always says I've got a temper on me. She says I ought to learn to control it."

I muttered, "That's OK."

"It's not OK!" Millie bounced herself down, rather crossly, on to a cushion. "I oughtn't to have said what I said."

"If you mean about me making myself sick—"

"Not that! Though you *did*."

I didn't attempt to argue. I didn't even mention the yoghurt. I knew that she was right.

"It was all the other stuff," said Millie. "Telling you to get a grip, and saying you were pathetic. I only did it cos I was so angry! And hurt, as well," she added, "if you want to know the truth."

I bit my lip, not knowing what to say. It was Millie who'd told them about Charlie being my sister! I was the one that ought to be hurt.

"Thing is, I didn't *do* anything," said Millie. "You accused me of something without ever bothering to ask me if I was guilty. You just took other people's word for it. It's not what friends are supposed to do."

I stared at her, horrified. "You mean, Zoe was telling lies?"

"What did she say, exactly?"

"It was Lola," I mumbled. "She said, we know she's your sister cos Millie O'Dowd said she was."

"*Said* she was. Not *told* us she was."

I wasn't quite sure that I could see the difference, though I really did want to.

"Shall I tell you what *actually* happened?" said Millie. I nodded humbly. "We were standing there, watching, and Charlie kept scoring all these goals, and this girl in Year 9, at least I think she's in Year 9, said, 'That's Charlie McBride – I used to be at primary school with her.' So then Zoe, all loud and clanging, like the girl had been talking to *her*, which she hadn't, said, 'She wouldn't be Peaches McBride's sister, would she?' And the girl said yes, she was, and Zoe and the others started on about how no one would ever have thought it and how you weren't in the least bit alike, blah blah blah, so that's when I got mad and told them that Charlie was useless and spoilt and your mum had to run after her all the time, and—" Millie broke off and waved a hand. "I just told them what I thought."

She'd been sticking up for me. Being my *friend*. I swallowed another hard-boiled egg.

"Probably I should have kept my mouth shut," said Millie, "but I just can't stand that Zoe!"

I agreed that I couldn't stand her either. "She can be really mean."

"She's not just mean, she's snobby. *And* she thinks she's the cream of the cream! Which she most definitely is not. More like cream gone sour. *Yuck!*"

I said, "Double yuck."

"Bleuuuurgh!" Millie looked at my books spread out on the floor. "What you up to?"

I said, "Nothing much. Just trying to do my maths homework."

"Want some help?"

"Omigod, *please*," I said.

After Millie had patiently explained to me what it all meant – she wouldn't ever *do* it for me; she said it was important that I understood – we settled cosily side by side on our cushions.

"Other reason I got so angry," said Millie, "it wasn't just you taking Zoe's word without even bothering to ask me, it was cos it drives me nuts when you keep putting yourself down all the time. Like the rest of your family are so much better than you are? Just cos they're all loud and noisy and convinced they're something special?"

I blinked. Was Millie being critical? Of my family? Everybody loved my family! They wrote about them, they interviewed them, they took photographs of them. They *were* something special!

"What gets me," said Millie, "it's the way you go along with it. Like they're royalty, or something! It's this stupid habit you've got into. Thinking you're *Just Peachy* and they're all geniuses. I mean, I know your Dad's a bit of a celeb and your brother writes music, but so what? You're just as good as they are! Better than some of them, if you ask me. Remember I told you I only make friends with people I find interesting? Well, I wouldn't find your sister Charlie interesting. I'd find her a total waste of space! Like she'd probably find me a dead bore. But know what? It wouldn't bother me one little bit! I don't *care* what people like her think about me. I don't care what people like Zoe think about me. And you shouldn't care what they think about you either!"

I heaved a sigh. "I know."

"So are you going to *stop* caring and do what you said you were going to do? Concentrate on being you?"

"I am trying," I said.

Millie clasped her hands together and looked at me over a pair of imaginary spectacles. In Sister Agatha's voice she said, "You must try harder, my dear."

That made me giggle, but all the same I couldn't help thinking it would be a lot easier if I could just find something I was any good at. Like when Mum said I had "my own thing". She'd been saying it for years, just to boost my confidence, but nobody, least of all me, had any idea what that thing was supposed to be. It worried me, sometimes, that maybe it didn't really exist. There wasn't any *thing*. I didn't say this to Millie though. I didn't want her thinking I was pathetic. Instead I asked her if she was looking forward to the Christmas party.

Enthusiastically Millie said, "Yes!"

I said, "Me too."

The party wasn't for us, but for pupils at Hill House, the special-needs school just down the road from Sacred Heart. Sister Agatha had impressed upon us that the Christmas party was one of Sacred Heart's most cherished traditions.

"One we are extremely proud of. And it's you people in Year 7 whom we rely on to keep that tradition alive. It's entirely up to you!"

We were to play hosts. Millie and I agreed that it was a big responsibility. They could have chosen Year 8s, or Year 9s, but they hadn't. They had chosen us. Zoe, in her know-it-all way, said, "It's always Year 7," like that meant we could stop congratulating ourselves cos it wasn't anything so wonderful. But we all felt that it was. We often saw the little special-needs kids playing in their school grounds, or being brought in by bus in the morning, some of them in wheelchairs, some of them needing to be helped, and we desperately wanted to give them a good time and make sure they enjoyed themselves. Zoe, again in her know-it-all way, said, "It's one kid for each of us. Then you have to stay with them and look after them and give them a hand eating and drinking." She made it sound as if it was a bit of a drag, like she'd rather not have anything to do with it.

"And it's up to Sister Agatha," she said, "which kid you're given. You don't get to choose. They don't ask you which you want, a boy or a girl. My cousin got this kid that couldn't move, hardly. It was like a nightmare! She didn't know what to do with him."

"I suppose it would be difficult," I said, as I sat there on my cushion next to Millie, "if you got some poor little kid that couldn't move?"

"Even more difficult for the poor little kid," said Millie.

I said, "Yes, but what I mean, I'd be scared I wasn't looking after them properly."

Millie thought about it. "I don't reckon Sister Agatha would put you with someone if she didn't feel you were up to it."

"She did with Zoe's cousin!"

"Yeah, well. *Zoe*." Millie screwed up her face. "I wouldn't trust anything *she* said."

I agreed. You couldn't trust *anything* Zoe said. Anyway, I didn't want to think about Zoe. She had almost managed to come between me and Millie. Rearranging myself cross-legged on my cushion, I said, "I can't believe we've been at Sacred Heart almost a whole term. Can you?"

"D'you remember when we started?" said Millie. "That first day? Zoe and her politics of envy!"

"And you saying how people thought bus drivers were greedy for wanting more money."

"I couldn't resist it," said Millie. "That girl *really* rubs me up the wrong way!"

We sat happily chatting until it was time for Millie to go.

"I'm really sorry I thought you'd told them about Charlie," I said.

"I'm really sorry I got mad at you," said Millie.

We were friends again!

I was growing quite excited at the thought of the Christmas party. I'd seen one or two really sweet little kids in the Hill House playground. One little girl in particular. She was in a wheelchair, but she was always so bright and happy. If only Sister Agatha would choose her for me to look after! I had these visions of helping her unwrap her present, which might be a doll perhaps, so we could talk about what she was going to call her; or maybe it would be a picture book, and we'd go through it together, with me reading the words. I'd really enjoy that!

The day of the party arrived and I rushed down to eat breakfast and get off to school, ready to help set up the gym with the Christmas tree and the pressies.

"You're looking very bright-eyed and bushy-tailed," said Mum.

It's not very often Mum notices how I'm looking. Eagerly I told her that today was the Christmas party.

"What Christmas party?" Mum seemed surprised. "Whose Christmas party?"

"At school," I said. "I told you about it, ages ago!"

"Sorry," said Mum. "Obviously in one ear and out the other. Charlie, what's the matter? What are you after?"

"My contact lenses!" Charlie snatched up a saucepan that was on the draining board and peered into it distractedly. "I've lost them!"

"How can you lose contact lenses?"

"I was going to put them in and then I went and did something else and forgot!"

"So where did you leave them?"

"I don't know! Out here."

"On the *draining* board?"

"I don't know!"

Mum sighed and went over to the sink.

"It's something that happens every year," I said.

Coop gave a loud guffaw. "What, her losing her contact lenses?"

"The party! It's for little kids with special needs. We have to look after them and make sure they're having a good time.

"That's nice," said Mum, peering into the waste bin. "I hope you didn't go and throw them out with the rubbish."

"As one does," said Coop.

"You shut up!" screeched Charlie. She spun round to the twins. "What are you giggling for?"

Nobody ever knows what the twins are giggling for. They just giggle.

"Everybody stop what they're doing," said Mum, "and look for Charlie's contact lenses."

They finally turned up in the food cupboard, next to a tin of biscuits.

"*Now* I remember," said Charlie. "I put them there to be safe while I got myself a glass of milk."

"That makes sense," agreed Coop.

Charlie glared at him. "I'm going to go and put them in," she said, "and then I'm ready. I need to be at school really early today – we've got a special hockey practice." She went whisking out into the hall.

"I've got to be early too," I said. "We have to set up for the party. I'm just *so* hoping I get to look after this one little girl, she's so sweet, Mum! She—"

"Hang on a second," said Mum. "Charlie!" She called up the hall after her. "Make sure you don't forget your hockey boots this time! I don't want to have to come back and get them for you. Sorry, darling. What were you saying? Something about a little girl?"

"It's all right." I shook my head. "It doesn't matter." There just wasn't any point, trying to compete with Charlie.

"You were hoping you'd get to look after her?"

"Honestly, it's not important," I said. "I probably won't get her anyway."

At school we spent all morning arranging the gym. Mr Eccles, the school caretaker, climbed up his ladder and hung long strings of glittery stuff from the wall bars right across to the windows, while we decorated the tree with tinsel and glass ornaments and little paper lanterns. There was even an angel to go on the top. All round the foot of the tree were presents, pink-wrapped for the girls and blue for the boys.

"A bit sexist," grumbled Millie, but even she had to agree that most boys probably wouldn't thank you for a doll, or for what Coop (to annoy Charlie) calls girly stuff, meaning hair slides and bangles and 'little itty-bitty things'.

I said, "I bet the Diddy People like itty-bitty things."

Millie admitted that they did.

"I quite like them myself," I said.

Millie glanced over her shoulder. "Me too, but don't tell anyone!"

At two o'clock the children arrived from Hill House. There were twenty-eight of them, the same number as in our year, all aged between seven and nine. I saw my little girl – I'd started to think of her as mine – staring round, wide-eyed with wonderment, at all the decorations. In spite of telling myself that I wouldn't be chosen as her carer, I couldn't help secretly hoping. I stood, with fingers crossed, as people were paired off. At last it was my turn. There were six children left, including my little girl.

"Peaches!" Sister Agatha beckoned me over. "Peaches, this is Ben. Ben, this is Peaches. She's going to be taking care of you this afternoon."

My heart sank. Ben was one of the older ones. He was *big*. Big and ungainly. Slumped in his wheelchair, his head on one side.

Sister Agatha squeezed my shoulder. "I needed someone special," she said. "Someone who understands about boys." She smiled kindly. "I know you have two brothers!"

I gritted my teeth. *My family.* Always interfering. Always getting in the way. I'd thought by coming to Sacred Heart I might have escaped them.

Out of the corner of my eye I saw Sister Agatha lead Millie up to my little girl. Of course! Millie had three sisters. I tried not to be jealous, but I could feel the resentment boiling up. If I'd been a kettle, steam would have been bursting out of me.

I turned to look at this large ungainly boy that I was supposed to be taking care of. Thanks, Mum! Thanks, Dad! Just what I wanted.

And then the large ungainly boy flapped one of his hands at me and said, "Lo, Beedth."

At least, I think that's what he said. It was hard to be sure as his voice came out as a kind of harsh croak. But he plainly wanted me to shake his hand, so I stuck mine out and said, "Lo, Ben." Only then, at the last minute, instead of shaking hands I did a sort of high five. It obviously amused him, cos he made a gurgling sound and said, "Lo, Beedth," and flapped his hand again. So I said, "Lo, Ben," and did another high five.

"Lo, Beedth!"

"Lo, Ben!"

Zoe walked past helping a small girl who had callipers on her legs. (Had Zoe got sisters?) Her small girl wasn't nearly as sweet as my small girl, but anyone was better than a great lumping boy. Zoe looked from me to Ben and back to me again. Her expression was like, *Glad he's yours and not mine.*

So then *I* looked at Ben, and he gave me this lopsided smile, at least I think it was a smile, and waved his hand.

"Lo, Beedth!"

As I said, "Lo, Ben!" I suddenly felt ashamed of myself, taking out my resentment on some poor little kid. He might be big and lumping, but he was still only little in age. He deserved a good time! Far more than I did, for all my moaning and whinging. Cos really, when it came down to it, what did I have to complain about? Nothing! Not compared to Ben.

I squatted down next to his chair. "So what shall we do?" I said. "Do you want to stay in here with the others? Or shall we go outside?"

"Uddide!"

I said, "Outside?"

"**UDDIDE!**"

"Out there?" I pointed towards the door that led into the shrubbery. He didn't seem able to nod, but I could tell from the way his eyes lit up that that was what he wanted.

"Come on then," I said. "Let's go!"

I wasn't sure whether we were allowed to take our charges outside, but no one had specifically said that we couldn't, so I trundled us off and out through the door.

"Uddide!" cried Ben. He seemed quite excited.

Obviously I wouldn't have taken him if it had been freezing cold, or raining, but it was crisp and clear with only a tiny nip in the air, just enough to make you not want to stand around. By the time we'd slowly weaved in and out through the shrubbery I felt the moment had come for a bit of action.

"Want to go for a run?" I said. "Down there?"

I pointed at the long straight path which went along the side of the school. Ben gave a hoarse cry and flapped his hand. "Yedd!"

I said, "Right." I was beginning to understand him better by now. "Hang on!"

We charged off, Ben giving his loud harsh grunts, me going "Wheee!" as I bounced us over the gravel.

"Guess what?" I said. "We could be in training for the next Paralympics!"

He liked that idea. He beat with his fist on the arm of his chair and shouted it out: "Baralim!"

I joined in. "Para*lym*pics!"

"Baralim!"

We rocketed on, down the path. As we were approaching the gym, the door opened and Sister

Agatha stepped out. She was obviously looking for us. We screeched to a halt just centimetres away. Normally Sister Agatha would have been frosty, to say the least. We are not supposed to rush about like hoydens. (That is what she calls it: rushing about like hoydens.) Today all she said was, "Good gracious me, Peaches, what on earth is going on?" She didn't sound frosty at all. Almost more amused than anything. It was Ben who answered her. Very loudly he shouted, "**BARALIM**!"

I said, "We're in training, Sister. For the next Paralympics."

"I see." A ghost of a smile hovered on her lips, and then was gone. "Can I suggest you've probably done enough training for one day? Especially as it's time for tea."

"Tea!" I grabbed Ben's hand and slapped it again in a high five. His face lit up. "Let's go eat!" I said.

Ben was really messy when it came to eating. He spluttered and splurged and sprayed himself with crumbs. He sprayed me too, but I didn't mind. He was enjoying himself. What did a few crumbs matter? Or a bit of dribble. He couldn't help it.

Sitting opposite us were Millie and her little girl. The little girl was as neat as could be. She nibbled daintily and didn't spray or splutter at all. I wondered if I still felt resentful at having been paired with Ben, and discovered that I didn't. He beamed up at me, his face smeared with a mixture of jam and chocolate, and I wiped him clean with a paper hanky and he shouted, "Baralim!" and beat his fist on the arm of his chair.

"Can't do Paralympics now," I said. "You've got to open your present."

"Bredden?" He thumped again with his fist. "Bredden, bredden!"

"Look," I said, "this is your one... see? It's got your name on it – Ben Turpin. That's you, isn't it?"

He nodded eagerly. "Bredden!'

"Let's see what it is."

We opened it together. It seemed to be some kind of soft toy. Round and red and fluffy, with a smiley face and big sticky-out ears. Ben was entranced by it, especially when we discovered that by squeezing it you could make a sound like… well! I'm not sure I should say what the sound was like. 'Breaking wind' is the polite expression. That's what my gran would call it.

Everyone at the table turned to stare. You could tell that Ben liked having an audience cos he kept shooting these really cheeky glances at me and then *squeeeezing* as hard as he could and giving this loud throaty chuckle. Sister Agatha walked past and nodded benevolently.

"That's good," she said. "Good exercise. Keep it up!"

I must have looked a bit surprised — I mean, Sister Agatha actually *approving?* — cos she whispered, "For the hands. Good for the hands," as she moved on. And then I got what she meant. Ben didn't have much strength in his hands, so squeezing the fartball would help build up his muscles. (And I should like to state here and now that the expression *fartball* came from Millie. She said it without even blinking.)

At half past three the special bus arrived and the party was over. I wheeled Ben to the gates and kissed him goodbye. He insisted on kissing me back, a big wet slobbery kiss, and we gave each other a last high five. I thought that I was really going to miss him.

Sister Agatha was waiting as we went back into school. She said, "Well done, Peaches! You made one little boy very happy."

I danced on air the whole way home.

CHAPTER EIGHT

I couldn't wait to tell Mum about the party! About how I'd looked after Ben and how Sister Agatha had said well done. I suppose it was partly that I wanted to do a bit of boasting, cos it wasn't very often I had anything to boast about, but mainly it was because I was excited. I'd made one little boy very happy

– Sister Agatha had said so – and that had made *me* happy. I had really loved taking care of Ben, seeing his face light up, hearing his loud, happy laugh. I wanted to go on doing it! Could that mean I had at long last found something I was good at?

The minute I arrived home, the words came tumbling out of me.

"Mum, guess what? Sister A—"

"Oh, sweetheart, not right now!" Mum was flying out of the back door even as I burst in. "I have to go and pick Charlie up. I'm so glad you're home – can you hold the fort till I get back? Just keep an eye on the twins for me. I won't be long!"

With that, she was gone. I stood for a minute, all my excitement evaporating, then trailed into the house to find the twins watching television.

"Why does Mum have to go and pick Charlie up?" I said.

"Dunno," said Flora.

"Dunno," said Fergus.

"I thought she had an away match? I thought she wasn't going to be home till late?"

"Dunno," said Flora.

I stared at them, exasperated. "Didn't Mum *say?*"

"Said she's broken something." Fergus spoke without even bothering to take his eyes off the television screen.

"Broken what?" I said.

"Dunno," said Fergus.

"Neck?" said Flora.

"Broken her *neck?*" I almost screeched it.

"Ankle," said Fergus.

"Oh, yes. That was it." Flora nodded. "Broken her ankle."

"Or something."

"So where's Coop?"

"Dunno," said Flora.

"Dun—"

"Oh, forget it!" I said. Those twins really know how to annoy a person. They're spoilt rotten, that's the problem. Just because they're twins.

"We haven't had any tea yet," said Flora.

I said, "So what?"

"Aren't you going to get some for us?"

They both turned accusingly.

"You're supposed to be looking after us," said Flora.

"Oh, look after yourselves!" I snapped. "I've got better things to do."

"Like what?"

Flora's indignant wail followed me into the hall.

"None of your business," I said.

I was going to ring Gran. I had to tell *someone* my news, and Gran is always interested. What's more, she always has time to listen, unlike Mum.

"Hello, my darling!" Gran sounded surprised, but pleased. It is usually her ringing Mum, and Mum calling me to "have a word with your gran". She does occasionally call one of the others, but mostly it is me, cos me and Gran are special friends. "What's new?" she said. "What's going on in your life?"

"I think I may have discovered what I want to do!"

The words leapt out of my mouth, taking me unawares. "We've just had this Christmas party?" I gabbled. "Like at school, like every year? Like they invite these little special-needs kids and we're all given one to look after? So I had to look after this little boy – well, actually he wasn't that little, he was quite big, but he wasn't very old – and he was in a wheelchair, and he couldn't speak properly and just at first I found it really difficult to understand him, but then I got used to it, and Gran, we had such fun! Sister Agatha – she's this nun that's really strict – she told me I'd made him very happy, and I really, *really* enjoyed it, and I think that's what I'd like to do... work with special-needs children! Do you think I could?"

Gran said she was sure I could. She said, "That's wonderful! I'm so glad. Have you told your mum?"

"Mum's not here," I said. "She's had to go and pick Charlie up cos she's broken her ankle or something. In any case," I added, "Mum never really has time to listen."

Gran and I talked for simply ages. I'd only just put the phone down when Mum arrived home with Charlie, with her ankle all strapped up.

"Not broken," said Mum. "Just sprained."

"It's still *agony*," said Charlie. "Some idiot whacked me with her hockey stick!"

I didn't remind her that when she'd whacked me with *her* hockey stick she'd told me not to be such a wimp.

"The twins want some food," I said.

"Oh! You haven't fed them?" Mum made it sound like I ought to have done.

I said, "No, I was talking to Gran."

"Gran? Is she all right? She only rang yesterday."

"I rang her," I said. "I thought she'd like to hear about the party."

"Oh, your Christmas one! Of course, it was today, wasn't it? How did it go?"

"OK," I said.

"Good! That's good. Charlie, why don't you sit down

and rest that ankle? It won't get better if you keep hobbling round on it. Peachy, do you want to help me get some tea? We're not going to be eating till late tonight, so—"

"I don't need any," I said. "We had tea at school."

"Oh. All right! You could still help me get some for the others."

"I'll tell the twins," I said. "*They* can come and help."

"Get her!" jeered Charlie, as I left the kitchen.

If I had been Millie I would have made a rude gesture. As I'm not, I just went "Hmph!" and tossed my hair back over my shoulder. Even worms can turn.

On Monday at school we eagerly discussed the party, swapping stories about how it had gone and what we'd done.

"But poor old you," said Zoe.

I said, "Me?"

"Getting one like that."

"Like what?" I said.

Zoe flopped her head to one side, letting her eyes go crossed and her tongue loll out. I felt a sort of blind rage boil up inside me. I don't think I have ever come so close to hitting someone. It was Millie, in this icy voice, who said, "What's that supposed to mean?"

"Well – you know! Not quite all there."

I said, "For your information, Ben is *absolutely* all there. Just cos a person has difficulty speaking doesn't mean they're an idiot."

"Even if it did," said Millie, "that's no reason they shouldn't be given a good time."

"Didn't say it was," said Zoe. "I was just feeling sorry for Peachy."

"Well, you don't have to," I snapped, "cos I enjoyed myself. So there!"

"You really did, didn't you?" said Millie, as we pointedly moved away from Zoe. "I could see that you were. I t—"

"Hey, Peaches!" We stopped and turned. A small

figure was scurrying towards us. Janine Corrie, otherwise known as the Mouse. "I just wanted to say, I thought you did brilliantly with Ben!"

"Do you know him?" I said.

"He lives right next door. I've known him for ever. I was sure I'd be asked to look after him! I was just *so* relieved when Sister Agatha picked you." The Mouse pulled a face, like she felt guilty admitting it. "Not that I wouldn't have done my best, but he can be really difficult when he wants."

"Like how?" said Millie.

"Like throwing tantrums, kind of thing?"

"He didn't throw any with me," I said.

"That's cos he liked you! You obviously knew how to get on with him."

Millie nodded triumphantly. "I told you Sister Agatha wouldn't put you with someone unless she felt you were up to it!"

It was a few days later when Mum said that Gran had called and had told her my news.

"She says you've decided you'd like to work with children with special needs. Is that right?"

I nodded, a bit shyly.

"Well, that's nice," said Mum. "It's good to have something to aim for. But how come your gran got to hear of it before me? Honestly, darling, you are so secretive! You never tell me anything!"

"I do try," I mumbled.

"I can't believe it's *that* hard," said Mum. "After all, I'm always here!"

I was about to point out that she was always *busy*, but before I'd even opened my mouth there was an anguished yell from Charlie, somewhere up on the landing, and Mum had gone whizzing off to see what the problem was.

"Speak later!" she cried. But of course we never did.

Two weeks before the end of term I had a really BIG surprise. Janine Corrie, that everyone called Mouse, gave me an invitation to her birthday party! She gave one to Millie as well.

"Wonders will never cease," said Millie.

She was making like she wasn't impressed, but I knew that she was. She had to be! The Mouse was one of the most popular girls in our class. Zoe might be the loudest and the most full of herself, and she did have one or two faithful followers such as Rhiannon and Lola, who attached themselves like they were stuck with superglue, but me and Millie weren't the only people who thought she was opinionated and snobby. Lots of the others didn't really like her. The Mouse was tiny and cheerful. Everybody loved the Mouse.

"She's probably gone and invited the whole class," said Millie.

But she hadn't. I'd seen her dishing out the invitations. I'd wondered what they were. I couldn't believe it when one had landed on my desk. The Mouse was inviting *me*?

I told Millie that we were the only two invited that

the Mouse hadn't been at Juniors with, to which Millie went, "Hmm!" Like she wasn't sure whether to believe me or not.

"I suppose she's asked old Big Mouth?"

She meant Zoe.

"She'd have to," I said. "She went to hers."

"What, to old Big Mouth's?" Millie pulled a face.

"Don't you want to go?" I said.

"Oh, I'll *go*," said Millie. And then she grinned and said, "Never turn down an invitation to a party!"

"Especially this one," I said. "I heard there are going to be *boys*."

"Oh, wow!" Millie went into a pretend swoon. "*Boys!*"

"Yes, well," I said. "You were the one complaining we never meet any."

Earlier in the term we'd earnestly assured each other we didn't think boys were all that important. We could live without them! I'd told Millie how Mum had been worried that going to an all girls school might not be such a good idea.

"Doesn't bother *me*," I'd said.

Millie had agreed. "Me neither!"

Boys! Who needed them?

Nothing had specially happened to change our minds. It was just this strange feeling that had begun to creep over us. Not that we actually *needed* boys. But maybe, every now and again, it might be interesting to meet one.

"At least you have brothers," grumbled Millie.

I said that they didn't count. "They're not normal. None of my family's normal."

"They're still boys," said Millie.

"Sort of," I said.

Millie giggled at that. "How can they be *sort of*?"

I told her that Coop was too busy being a genius and that Fergus was too busy being a twin. "What we need are some *real* boys."

"You mean, not just sort-of boys."

"I mean ordinary, everyday ones."

"Dunno where you find any of them," said Millie.

I was about to say, "At the Mouse's party?" But my eyes had flickered down to the invitation and suddenly I'd seen something. "Oh!"

"What?" said Millie. "What's the problem?"

She had obviously caught the note of anguish in my voice.

"I'm not going to be able to go!"

"What do you mean, you won't be able to go? Why not?"

"It's on the nineteenth. That's Dad's birthday!"

Millie looked at me doubtfully. "You mean, like, he has a party or something?"

"No – well, he does have a party, but that's later." That was at New Year's. Dad's big birthday bash, when loads of his and Mum's friends came and partied through the night.

"So…?" Millie said it carefully. I could tell that she was trying hard to understand. My family is very different from hers, and I know it is not always easy.

"We all go out to dinner," I said. "Mum likes everyone to be there."

Millie crinkled her nose. "You're always going out to dinner!"

"Yes, I know," I said. I felt a bit ashamed, having to admit it. We sometimes went out as many as two or three times a week. It suddenly didn't seem quite right. Not when there were people starving and living on the street. "It is Dad's birthday," I pleaded.

"All the same," said Millie. "How's it any different from all the other times you go?"

She wasn't getting at me. At least, I didn't think she was. She was just curious to know. But the more I thought about it, the more I realised I didn't have an answer. How *was* it any different? It wasn't! It was true that we went to this really posh, expensive restaurant called La Cigale, which was Mum and Dad's favourite place in the whole wide world and charged like a small fortune just for a roll and butter, but then we went there on Mum's birthday as well, and we went there whenever there was anything extra special to celebrate, like Dad winning an award or Coop having his music performed or Charlie getting her name in the local paper. It wasn't exactly unusual, going to La Cigale. Like it wasn't unusual for Dad to order a bottle of champagne or smoke a big fat cigar.

"Would it so terribly matter," said Millie, "if you weren't there?"

"If I didn't go?"

"Yes! If you didn't go."

Even just the thought of it startled me. How could I not go to Dad's birthday dinner? We always went to Dad's birthday dinner! All of us. It was a family tradition.

"You'll be there at New Year's," said Millie, "won't you?"

I nodded slowly.

"So would they really mind if just this once..." Her voice trailed off. "Which would you *rather* do?"

I said, "Go to Mouse's party!"

 174 ☆

I'd said it before I could stop myself. It did seem a bit disloyal to Mum and Dad, but it honestly *wasn't* like we did anything special at La Cigale. Just sat down and ate, the same as usual. Everybody talking at the tops of their voices, also the same as usual. And me sitting there being Just Peachy. Same as usual. The chances were, they wouldn't even miss me. Maybe halfway through the evening someone would say, "Hey, we're one short! Who's not here?" And someone else would say, "Oh, it's just Peachy." And then they would all go surging back to their talking and their eating.

"Do they always expect you to go?" said Millie. "I mean, like, all of you? Always?"

"Well, Coop didn't go one year," I said. "But that was only cos he was studying for some special music exam. And last year Charlie couldn't be there cos she was on holiday with a friend. Oh, and one year the twins—"

I broke off. Millie was looking at me.

"What?" I said.

"Listen to yourself!" cried Millie.

"What?" I said. "What?"

"*Coop* didn't go, *Charlie* didn't go, *the twins* didn't go."

"Yes, but that was only cos—"

"Cos what?"

"Cos they were going to the pantomime that afternoon with Gran, and Mum said they'd get crabby." I heard myself mumbling it. Millie was still looking at me.

"It was two years ago," I muttered. "They were only little."

"So you're the only one that's *always* gone."

There was a silence while I thought about it.

"Where's the difference between Charlie going on holiday and you going to a party?" Millie sounded quite aggressive. "It's not fair!" she said. "I don't think your family *are* fair. Not to you they're not. Oh, Peachy, do come! I can't go by myself."

I didn't ask her why she couldn't. She obviously could. It wasn't like she was shy or anything. But I *so* didn't want her to! I hated the thought of missing out. Having to hear everything second-hand. I wanted to *be* there. My very first party since I'd started at Sacred Heart. I *couldn't* not go!

"Peachy?" Millie was pleading with me now. "Think of all the boys we'll meet… *real* boys. Normal, everyday boys. We're nearly twelve years old and we still don't know any. If we don't start soon it'll be too late. We won't know how to talk to them or… or how to behave with them, or… anything!"

I took a deep breath. "You're right," I said.

"I know I'm right. It's getting desperate!"

"We'll turn into weirdos," I moaned.

"We practically *are* weirdos."

"We are! We're weirdos!"

Almost twelve years old, and we didn't know a single solitary boy. It was frightening.

"So are you going to come?" said Millie.

"Yes!" My mind was made up: I was going to go. No matter what Mum and Dad said. I knew they wouldn't be happy, but I had to make a stand. If Charlie could do it, so could I!

"I'll tell them tonight," I said.

CHAPTER NINE

We had dinner at home that evening. Coop had made his famous risotto with red peppers. Coop is ace at cooking. We all reckon that if it weren't for being a musical genius he could become a famous TV chef and run his own restaurant. And then, says Mum, we could all eat out every night at his place.

She said it again as we tucked into the risotto. "No more arguments about where to go – it'll be Chez Coop every time!"

"If you think," said Dad, "that I would ever patronise an establishment called Chez Coop—"

"Chez le Maestro?"

Dad shuddered. "Forget it! I'm a creature of habit. La Cigale is my spiritual home. I hope you've booked the table?"

"I have," said Mum. "I've told Gaston to expect the whole tribe… I told him, it's the big one this time. The big four-o!"

"Four-o's not all that big," said Fergus.

"Seems pretty big to me," said Dad.

"Wait till you're *five*-o," said Flora. "That's big!"

Dad shook his head. "I'm not sure there's life after that one."

"Oh, Alastair, for heaven's sake," said Mum, "don't be so absurd! Fifty's nothing these days."

"Nicholas Clooney's dad is over seventy," said Fergus.

"Phew!" Flora rolled her eyes. "That's ancient! For a dad."

"Ancient for anyone," said Dad.

"I don't expect," said Fergus kindly, "you'll be able to get about much by then?"

"Very likely not," agreed Dad. "Which is why I intend to make the most of it while I can." Dad beamed round happily. "All my family, gathered together, drinking a toast to the poor old decrepit man."

"I'll write you a special birthday dirge," said Coop. "Dirge in five voices. We'll serenade you as we toast!"

"What's a dirge?" Flora wanted to know.

"It's what you have at funerals. A burial song."

"*Burial?*" Flora's eyes went big. "What are we burying?"

"Dad's youth," said Charlie. "Let's do it now. Let's have a rehearsal!"

"OK, I can't manage the words, but something like this…" Coop pinched his nose between finger and thumb and began making a desolate droning noise. Charlie and the twins immediately joined in.

"Come on, come on!" Coop gestured impatiently at me, across the table. "*Five* voices!"

Reluctantly I pinched my nose and started droning. I was going to have to say something. Coop, being Coop, really *would* write his birthday dirge. He would expect us all to learn our parts and turn in a polished performance. We were the McBrides! When we did things, we did them properly.

I waited till we'd all finished droning.

"Dad," I said, "would you mind terribly if—"

A penetrating screech suddenly drowned me out: it was Charlie, bursting into song.

"*Four-o! The big four-o!*"

Coop at once took it up, followed by the twins, in their shrill treble voices.

"Peachy?" Coop kicked at me, under the table. "*Four-o...*"

"*The big four-o...*" I carolled it obediently.

"Oh, this will be great!" Mum clapped her hands. "I can't wait to see Gaston's face!"

"The only thing is," I said, "I—"

"*Peachy!*"

We were going round for a second time.

"I'm not going to be there!" I squawked.

Omigod, it was like shouting, **"FIRE!"** all over again. Well, the shouting part. Trying to make myself heard. At least this time though, they took notice. The singing stopped, abruptly.

"You what?" said Coop.

"I'm not going to be there!"

"Not going to *be* there?"

"Whoa!" Dad set down his wine glass. "How can you not be there? It's my birthday!"

"His big four-o!"

"I'll be there at New Year's," I pleaded. I sounded pathetic, like a sheep bleating. I didn't know which I was more scared of: Millie, or my family. I knew that Millie would never forgive me if I backed down. But she had no idea how unnerving it was, sitting there with all those accusing eyes boring into me.

"This is ridiculous!" said Coop. "It's a five-part harmony. I need five voices!"

"You could always use Mum," I quavered.

"Oh, no!" Mum very firmly shook her head. "I shall be the big four-o myself in a few months' time."

I didn't quite see how that should stop her taking my place, but Coop said no, a mature voice would totally unbalance everything.

"So maybe we could record it," I said.

"It's supposed to be live!" roared Charlie. "We all stand up and we *sing*!"

I thought, *who said?* But I didn't actually say it. I was in enough trouble already. Charlie is fond of laying down the law. She is not used to anyone rebelling, and specially not me.

"We don't *lip* sync." She said it scornfully. "We *perform*."

I muttered that they could perform just as well without me.

"But it's a five-part harmony!" Coop sounded like he was in actual pain.

"You can't back out now," said Flora. "It would be unprofessional. Wouldn't it?" She turned, self-righteously, to Mum. "Tell her it would be unprofessional!"

"Yes, yes, totally unprofessional. What I don't understand," said Mum, "is *why* you're not going to be there?"

I swallowed. "Cos I've been invited to a party?"

"What party?"

"Girl in my class?"

"You mean, Minnie?"

"No, another girl."

For a minute I almost thought Mum was going to say, "You know *another* girl?" Like she couldn't believe anyone else would ever invite me to anything.

"Are you telling me," said Dad, "that this is more important than helping a poor decrepit old man celebrate his birthday?"

I squirmed. It would be hard to imagine anyone *less* decrepit than Dad. He looks like a member of the English rugby team and he bellows like a bull. But he knows how to make a person feel bad.

"Imagine, I might not be here for the next one," he said.

"Oh, Alastair, stop it!" said Mum.

"I'm just saying."

"Well, don't!"

"But it's his big four-o," said Charlie. "And Coop's doing a five-part harmony!"

I had a sudden flash of inspiration. "Shouldn't it be a *four*-part harmony? I mean, if it's the big *four-o*…?"

There was a silence. I could see Coop turning it over in his mind. The others, I think, were a bit stunned. They don't expect that sort of smart remark from me.

It was Mum who recovered first.

"Oh, do your own thing," she said. "Far be it from

me and your dad to force you. If this is what you want..."

She waited for me to say that it wasn't. That I'd had a change of heart. *Of course* I would be at Dad's birthday dinner!

But I forced my lips to stay glued together, and said nothing. I could hear Millie's voice in the background: *Way to go!*

Mum pursed her lips. Dad, with a heavy sigh, reached out for the wine bottle. "I knew it would come to this – a man gets old and his loving children start ignoring him."

"*We're* not ignoring you!" shrilled Flora.

"Oh, it will happen," said Dad. "It will happen."

"Dad, it won't *ever*!" Flora jumped up and went rushing round the table to plant a kiss on Dad's cheek. "Me and Fergus will always love you!" She shot a sly glance at me. "*Always!*"

Later that evening Millie texted me: Did U do it?

I texted back: Yes.

Seconds later, she rang me on my mobile. "So what happened?"

"I told them about the Mouse's party and Mum said if that was what I wanted to do, I'd better do it."

"Yay!" Millie's glad cry came joyfully bouncing down the telephone. "They didn't mind too much, did they?"

I didn't know what to say to that.

"Peachy? You don't sound very happy."

That was because I wasn't. I was proud that I'd spoken up for once, and not let myself be bullied, but it didn't make me feel good. Shortly after talking to Millie I heard Mum coming upstairs.

"Mum?" I stuck my head round my bedroom door.

"I'm going to have a soak in the bath," said Mum.

She made it sound like it was something she needed after my selfish behaviour. Like I'd given her a headache.

"Mum, I'm really sorry," I said. "But I will be there at New Year's!"

"Oh, Peachy, we've been through all this," said Mum.

"You'd rather go to a party than be with your dad on his birthday. Enough said."

I called after her as she disappeared into the bathroom. "What about last year?"

Mum came back out on to the landing. "What about last year?"

"When Charlie didn't go."

"Charlie was in Switzerland," said Mum.

"On *holiday*."

"So?"

I felt like saying, "If she could go on holiday, I can go to a party." But I wasn't quite brave enough.

"What about Coop?" I said. "That time he didn't go? And the twins!"

"The *twins?*"

"When Gran took them to the pantomime the same afternoon as Dad's birthday and we had to leave them at home with a babysitter cos you said they'd get crabby."

"They would have done," said Mum. "Believe me!"

"So why couldn't Gran take them on a different day? Why did it have to be Dad's birthday? If it's that important?"

Mum was staring at me like I'd taken leave of my senses. She said, "What is all this? What's come over you all of a sudden? I'm beginning to regret I ever let you go to Sacred Heart if this is what it does to you!"

"It's nothing to do with Sacred Heart," I said.

"Then what is it to do with?"

"I just—"

"What? Tell me!"

"I just so, *so* want to go to this party!"

"Well, go," snapped Mum. "Who's stopping you?"

With that, she swished into the bathroom and closed the door. I'd never known her so upset before. I didn't have the feeling that Dad terribly cared one way or the other, so long as I was there for New Year's, and it hardly made any difference to Charlie and the twins. Even Coop had calmed down now that he'd decided four voices would do as well as five. But Mum was *really* cross. She is very protective of Dad, which is odd when you think he spends most of his life shouting at people on the radio and being rude to them. You wouldn't imagine he would need any protecting. But Mum is fiercely loyal. I guess after all these years she must still be in love with him.

I stood for a moment, dithering, then crept along the landing and called rather nervously to her through the bathroom door, "I will come if you really want me to."

"Oh, go away," said Mum. "You've disappointed me."

I didn't dare admit to Millie next day that I'd nearly caved in. All it would have taken was for Mum to come out of the bathroom and hug me and say, "Oh, darling, that would make me so happy!" And there I'd be, not going to the party. But Mum had been too cross. I had let her down. I had let the whole family down. It was the biggest crime you could commit.

I really hated being in Mum's bad books. I found it difficult to match Millie's enthusiasm when she wanted to joke about all the boys we'd meet, and discuss what we were going to wear, and whether I should go back to her place afterwards and spend the night.

"Cos maybe your dad won't want to come and pick you up, if he's in the middle of dinner?"

I agreed that he probably wouldn't. The party was due to finish at nine, and we never left La Cigale till at least half past ten.

Millie said, "Great! It's time we had another sleepover."

She was full of plans. Her dad would pick us up afterwards, and if I liked they could call and collect me beforehand.

"Then we could go together! That would be fun, wouldn't it?"

I agreed that it would, but she must have detected a slight note of doubt in my voice.

"You're having second thoughts!" she cried.

"I'm not," I said, "honestly."

"You are," wailed Millie. "Oh, Peachy, please, *please* don't let them talk you out of it! Promise me you won't!"

"I won't," I said. "I promise.

It is so easy to make promises. So difficult, sometimes, to keep them. I wavered, back and forth. One minute I was defiant: I *would* go to the party! The next, I felt that I just couldn't bear it any longer; I would do anything to make Mum happy!

It was Gran, as so often, who came to my rescue. I'd heard Mum talking to her on the telephone and guessed from the tone of her voice she was telling her all about me and my selfish behaviour. I so didn't want to accidentally catch what she was saying that I ran upstairs and shut myself in my room. When Mum called up to me, "Peachy, do you want a word with your gran?" I was reluctant to go back down. I dreaded the thought that now Gran was going to be cross with me as well.

I said, "Lo, Gran."

"What's all this I hear?" said Gran, and my heart just sank. "You've been invited to a party? Someone in your class?"

I went, "Mm."

"Excellent! I know your mum isn't pleased with you, but I do hope you're going to go?"

I think my mouth must have dropped open, cos I couldn't get any words out. Gran was *encouraging* me?

"Don't let them make you feel guilty. You go, and enjoy yourself! They all have fun, doing their own thing. Now it's your turn."

"But Mum thinks I'm being selfish," I said.

"Not before time, either."

"But it's Dad's birthday!"

"So what?" said Gran. "He's not a child. You'll be there for his big bash! That's what really matters to him. Having you all there, showing you off to his friends. Not singing some silly dirge in the middle of a restaurant, which I might say is *very* bad manners. Not everyone wants to hear the McBrides in full flood! Furthermore – " Gran said this bit rather tartly – "I don't seem to recall all this anguish when your sister wasn't there for his actual birthday."

"But she was in Switzerland," I bleated. I kind of felt duty bound to stick up for Mum. "I'm only going to a party!"

There was a pause, then Gran said, "When was the last time you went to one?"

"Dunno." I wrapped one leg round the other and stood there like a stork.

"Some months ago," said Gran, "as I recall. So this is every bit as important to you as going to Switzerland was to your sister. Maybe even more. I know it's not easy for you, sweetheart, but you must stand up for yourself, otherwise that family of yours will just overwhelm you."

I sighed and unwrapped my leg. "That's what Millie says."

"In that case," said Gran, "you just make sure you listen to her. And you can tell her I said so!"

CHAPTER TEN

Since speaking to Gran, Mum wasn't anywhere near as cross with me as she had been. She even suggested, the Saturday before we broke up from school, that maybe I should buy myself something special to wear to the party.

"Why don't you pop down to Gina's?" she said.

Gina is one of Mum's friends from school. She has a shop in the indoor market where she sells everything from bangles and bracelets to floaty skirts and sequinned tops, along with jeans and jackets, and belts and beads, and scarves and sandals, and just about whatever else you might want.

"Go down there this morning," said Mum, "and find something you like. Just make sure it's pretty!"

If I had been Charlie, I would have rolled my eyes. Charlie isn't into pretty: she is into *style*. Sometimes it is style that Mum approves of; sometimes it isn't. She absolutely hated it when Charlie went through a phase of nineties grunge and started wearing shredded shorts and big boots and a top that looked like it had been knitted out of barbed wire. She has never needed to worry about me, cos to be honest I am not hugely fashion conscious. I do care about clothes, but I wouldn't ever be bold enough to go round in some of the gear that Charlie wears, even if it is the height of fashion. Charlie is one of those massively confident people that can get away with shredded shorts and barbed wire. Me, I am more a fading-into-the-background sort of person.

Mum asked me if I'd rather she went with me to Gina's, but I said no, I'd give Millie a ring and see if she would like to come.

"Good idea," said Mum.

Millie and me had never been shopping together before and clothes were not something we ever really talked about. I'd kind of assumed that Millie wasn't all that interested, but the minute we arrived at Gina's she took over, firmly telling me that "That wouldn't suit you" or "That's the wrong colour" or even, when I hopefully pulled out a puffy skirt with bright orange poppies on an emerald green background, "It's OK, but it's just not *you.*"

Humbly I asked her what was me.

"I'll know when I see it," said Millie. "Keep looking!"

Seconds later, she gave a triumphant cry. "*Here!*" She was waving a pair of skinny jeans at me. Black, with silver studs. "Peachy, you've got to have them! They're beautiful!"

They were beautiful, but they weren't my size.

"I'd never get into them," I wailed.

"Hang on, I might have some more out the back," said Gina. "Let me go and see."

"Oh, I do hope she has!" Millie was holding the jeans up against herself, in front of one of the long mirrors. "They're absolutely perfect!"

"Yes, if you're size zero," I said. Millie is practically size zero. Mum says she is like a sparrow. "Why don't you try them on? Then I can see what they look like."

"OK!"

It was all the invitation she needed. I knew she was dying to see if they fitted her. I gave her a push and she dived happily through the curtain into one of the tiny changing rooms. I crammed in with her.

"Look! See?" She twisted and turned in front of the mirror. "They'd really suit you!"

"They really suit *you*," I said.

"How are we doing?" Gina's head appeared round the edge of the curtain. "Here you go! Try these for size."

Oh, they were a perfect fit! I twisted and turned, trying to see myself from every angle.

"Was I right, or was I right?" Millie gestured at my image in the mirror. "God, I'd die for a pair of jeans like these!"

"So get them," I said. "We'll both get them! Then we can toss who wears them to the party."

Millie looked doubtful.

"Why not?" I said. I glanced at the price tag. "Your mum wouldn't mind, would she? They're not that expensive."

Millie pulled a face. "No, but the Diddy People have just had to have new shoes, and all the bills start coming in at this time of year."

They did? I had no idea. I wasn't even sure what bills she was talking about. But I did know that even if he was the cream of the cream, Millie's dad didn't earn anywhere near as much as my dad did, shouting at people on the radio.

"So, you gonna get them?" said Millie.

"Yes!" I suddenly decided: I was going to get them. I picked up both pairs and marched back across the shop.

"How were they?" said Gina.

I said, "Fine! I'd like this pair, please."

I laid them on the counter.

"*This* pair?" said Gina. "But they're the sm—"

"I know," I said quickly. "They're the ones I want."

Gina seemed doubtful. "Are you sure?" she said.

I nodded. I did so hope she wasn't going to warn me that they'd be too tight even if I did manage to wriggle my way into them.

"Well, if they don't quite fit," she said, handing me the bag, "you know you can always bring them back."

"Why does she think they wouldn't fit?" said Millie, as we left the market. "You've already tried them on."

"So've you," I said. "Here!" I thrust the bag at her. "They're yours."

"Mine?" Millie's face turned slowly crimson. I do believe it was the first time I had ever seen her blush. Even the tips of her ears were bright scarlet. "Peachy," she said, "you can't!"

I said, "Why not?"

"Because you – you just can't!"

"I can do whatever I like," I said.

"But what about your mum?"

"What about her?"

"She gave you the money to get something for *you*!"

"I don't need anything," I said. I wasn't being noble; it was quite true. I had a whole wardrobe full of stuff. "Look, just take them!" I said. "Don't be so... so..." I couldn't think of the word. "So *ungracious*."

She didn't say anything to that. Just stood there, frowning and chewing at her lip.

"We are supposed to be *friends*," I reminded her. "Friends do this sort of thing."

"But, Peachy," she said, "I really c—"

"Just take them!" I roared.

I could tell she was tempted. She'd really fallen in love with those jeans! I could see the struggle going on inside her. And then, miserably, she pushed the bag back at me.

"I can't," she whispered.

"So what am I supposed to do with them?" I said. "They're far too small for me!"

"She said you could take them back."

"Why should I take them back? I bought them for *you*. But if you don't want them – " I yanked them out of the bag – "I'll go and rub them in the gutter and make them all muddy, then they'll be no good to anyone!"

Millie put a finger to her mouth and began to tear rather wildly at a dry bit of skin. She'd make herself bleed if she wasn't careful, going at it like that.

"I will," I said. "I mean it!"

For one horrible moment I thought she was going to let me do it.

"You could probably have them dry-cleaned," I said, "but Gina's not going to take them back. And I certainly can't wear them. Maybe I'll just let them *drop*—" I held them up, between finger and thumb. We'd had a lot of rain just lately and there were still puddles everywhere. Dirty puddles. *Oily* puddles. "D'you want me to?" I said.

"No!" Millie gave a shriek and lunged at me. "You'll ruin them!"

"That's the idea," I said.

"Oh, please," begged Millie. "Please, Peachy! Don't be silly."

"Well, don't you," I said. I put the jeans back in the bag and held it out to her. Quite meekly, she took it.

"I don't know what to say," she mumbled.

"You don't have to say anything," I said. "I told you, we're *friends*. It's what friends do."

"But I haven't even said thank you!"

I didn't want her to say thank you. She said it anyway.

"Thank you, Peachy, thank you, *thank* you!"

It was really embarrassing.

"Shut up," I said. I gave her a little shove. "I got them so you could look cool. All those boys that are going to be there…?"

"Nudge nudge, wink wink," said Millie.

"No, but seriously," I said.

"Seriously," said Millie. "What are *you* going to wear?"

"Dunno," I said. "Haven't thought about it. You could come back with me, if you like, and help me find something?"

That cheered her up. I was hoping she wouldn't feel so bad once she saw all the stuff I had in my wardrobe. I'd always kept it from her before. It made me feel guilty, me having so much and Millie having so little, not to mention starving children and people living on the streets.

"It's not right, is it?" I said, as I pulled open my wardrobe door.

Millie's jaw didn't exactly drop, but I could see she was shocked.

"I keep telling Mum I don't need any more clothes! I mean, some of them I've hardly ever worn. But she just keeps getting them."

It is Mum's firm belief that when it comes to clothes you can never have too many. I was always arriving home from school to find the dining room table covered in skirts and tops, and shoes and trousers, with Mum, giggling, a little shamefaced, and explaining how Gina had just had the new season's fashions come in. She would urge us to "Try them on, see what you think!"

She never brought stuff home for Coop or Fergus; just for me and Flora. Well, and for Charlie too, in the early days, but then Charlie had grown bold and started rebelling and saying she wouldn't be seen dead in anything so hideous, and Mum had sadly given up. I couldn't help wondering if it was time I started to rebel.

"Nobody should have all these clothes," I said. "Right?"

"It is kind of... obscene," agreed Millie.

I looked at her doubtfully. *Obscene?* Didn't that mean, like, porno, or something? She does use the strangest words.

"Do you think I should give some of it to Oxfam?" I said.

"It might make you feel better," said Millie.

"But would it do any good?"

"Wouldn't hurt."

"Let's do it!" I said. I reached in and began frantically unhooking hangers and chucking stuff on to the bed. "Let's go through it all and decide what I don't need."

By the time we'd finished we had a whole great pile of clothes waiting to be put into a black sack and taken down the road to the Oxfam shop.

"There!" I sank back on to my heels. "What do you think?"

Millie said, "Yes."

What did she mean, yes? She ought to be sounding more enthusiastic than that! I'd just cleared out half my wardrobe.

"You are going to check with your mum," she said, "aren't you?"

"Oh, she won't mind," I said. "She's always giving stuff away."

Millie said, "Hmm."

"Honestly," I said. "She buys stuff one day and gives it away the next. And look at all that lot! – I've still got loads left."

"So what are you going to wear?"

"You choose," I said.

"OK!"

Millie scrambled to her feet and sprang across to the wardrobe. After swishing hangers to and fro, and taking things out and holding them up and solemnly inspecting them, she settled for a top and a pair of trousers (both from Gina's) and insisted that I put them on so she could see how I looked.

She nodded approvingly. "Yes! That'll do. Makes you look nice and tall and slim."

"Ready for all those yummy boys we're going to meet."

I said it in a jokey kind of way, but the fact was we were both getting a bit obsessed by the thought of boys.

"Do you really reckon there'll be any?" I said.

"You bet! I asked the Mouse. I told her that was the only reason we were going."

"You didn't!?"

"Course I didn't!" Millie gave a happy cackle of laughter. "I just asked her if she'd really invited any and she said yes. She said there's going to be at least six. Ten of us and six of them. Maybe more if she can get them."

I said, "*More?*"

"More would be better," said Millie.

"But where does she get them all from?" How could anyone at an all-girls school manage to know *six boys*? *Real* boys?

Millie said, "Well, three of them are cousins. One's her brother. One's a friend of her brother. And one lives next door. Then maybe people might bring some with them, like if they have brothers or something... like you could bring yours, if you wanted."

"Coop?" I said, startled. "He wouldn't want to come."

"You mean, you wouldn't want him to!"

It had never occurred to me. But anyway, he couldn't. "He'll be at Dad's birthday dinner," I said.

"Oh!" Millie fanned herself. "What a relief!"

She was teasing me, I knew. She'd said just the other day that now my big secret was out I didn't have to keep my family hidden any more.

"I s'pose he'll be there at *your* birthday party?" she said.

Had she really turned a bit pink, or was I imagining it?

"Don't know if I'll have one," I said.

"You'd better!" said Millie.

Really, she was becoming dreadfully bossy. I sprang up, scattering clothes in all directions.

"Let's go get something to eat," I said.

Coop and the twins were in the kitchen. No Mum. I asked Coop where she was.

"Dunno." He was busy helping himself to biscuits. "Taking Charlie somewhere."

I said, "Oh." And then, remembering my manners, "Millie, this is my brother Coop."

"And I'm Peachy's friend Millie," said Millie.

Coop said, "Yeah. Hi."

"And we're the twins," said Fergus.

Crushingly I said, "She's already had the doubtful pleasure of meeting you."

"You don't have to be rude," said Flora. "We were just trying to make conversation."

Coop, edging out of the door with a can of Coke in one hand and a fistful of biscuits in the other, was stopped in his tracks by Millie.

"If Peachy has a birthday party, you will come to it, won't you?" she said.

A glazed look appeared in Coop's eyes. He

★ 212 ☆

said, "Yeah. Right," and shot sideways out of the door.

"I think you frightened him," I said.

"Didn't frighten us," boasted Fergus. "We'll come to your birthday party."

"Dunno that you'll be invited," I said.

"We'll come anyway," said Flora. "We like parties." She turned to Fergus. "Don't we?"

"Love 'em," said Fergus.

With that, they both dissolved into peals of mad giggles and followed Coop out of the room.

"Now look what you've done," I told Millie. "Who wants them to come?"

"It would be an extra boy," said Millie.

I said, "Huh! Call that a boy?"

"Coop is."

This time there was no mistaking it: she had turned bright pink.

"Omigod!" I said. "You haven't gone and fallen for him?"

She had! I could tell.

"Honestly," I grumbled, "I knew I should never have let you set eyes on him."

Mum and Charlie arrived home shortly after I'd seen Millie up the road to her bus stop.

"Hello!" said Mum. "What's in the black sack?"

"Clothes," I said. "For Oxfam. I've been having a clear-out."

"Really?" Mum opened the sack and peered in. "Oh, Peachy!" She pulled out a particularly repulsive blue dress that I had never worn. "You can't give this away!"

"Dead right," said Charlie. "Who'd take it?"

"But it's pretty!" protested Mum.

Charlie made a loud vomiting noise. Before I knew it, I had made one too.

"Mum, it's disgusting," I said.

Mum sighed. "Oh, well, have it your own way. I take it you found something to your liking at Gina's?"

"Something *pretty*," said Charlie.

"Where is it?" said Mum. "Let's have a look."

I said, "Um…"

"Well? Come on!" said Mum. "Let me see it."

Charlie gave a shrill cackle of laughter. "Obviously *not* pretty!"

"Oh, Peachy," said Mum. "You haven't gone all grungy, have you?"

I swallowed. "The thing is…"

"What?" said Mum.

"The thing is I – I didn't actually buy anything. For me. I thought about it and I decided I had quite enough clothes already and that it would be obscene to buy any more."

Mum blinked. Even Charlie broke off what she was doing and turned to stare.

"I take it," said Mum, "that you did buy *something*? Or did you put the money in a charity box?"

"Um… well… n-no. Not exactly," I said. "I – um – bought something for Millie."

"You bought something for Millie?"

There was a pause.

"She needed something," I pleaded. "For the party. Mum, she doesn't have many clothes and there are going to be boys and—"

"Oh, swoon!" said Charlie. "*Boys!*"

"Well, there are," I said. "And it's not fair if she can't look nice, cos I've got so much and she's got hardly anything and – and I thought you wouldn't mind if I… if I…"

My voice trailed away.

"You thought I wouldn't mind," said Mum, "if you spent the money on buying something for someone else."

"Um – well," I said. "Yes."

"I see."

Long silence. Charlie rolled her eyes and went back to whatever it was she was doing. Texting, from the look of it. I waited nervously for Mum to say something. At the time, when I'd gone marching up to the counter and told Gina which pair of jeans I wanted, it had seemed absolutely the right thing to do. The *only* thing to do. It hadn't even crossed my mind that Mum might look at it rather differently. Somehow, standing there in front of her, it suddenly seemed all too likely. Millie might be my friend – my very *best* friend – but that didn't mean I had the right to go spending Mum's money on her. I could see that now. I'd just got a bit carried away.

"I'm sorry," I muttered.

Mum shook her head. "Strange girl," she said. "Go and put that bag of clothes in the garage, I'll take them in tomorrow."

I grabbed the bag and ran. Mum is really surprising at times. I guess as mums go she has to be pretty special, even if she doesn't always properly listen or pay attention. Five children must be a lot for anyone to cope with, especially when two of them are twins and keep screeching with mad laughter for no apparent reason. Come to that, I should think Dad on his own must be a lot to cope with. Really, it's a wonder Mum is still sane.

I made a mental note to tell Gran next time we spoke: *Mum has a lot to cope with.* It seemed important that Gran should know.

CHAPTER ELEVEN

Saturday came: the day of the party. I was so excited I lay awake half the night thinking about it. Getting myself into a bit of a state, to tell the truth. It was ages since I'd been to a party! Last time had been way back at the beginning of Year 6, when we were still young enough to eat iced buns and jellies, and play games. I didn't imagine you would eat iced buns and jellies when you were in Year 7. Or play games. It would be, like, more teenage kind of stuff. Like dancing maybe, if there were boys. But I just wasn't sure.

Half way through the afternoon Millie texted to remind me that she and her dad were picking me up at seven o'clock, so *B redy!*

I immediately rang her. "Is seven o'clock early enough?"

Millie assured me that it was. "It'll only take ten minutes from your place."

"But seven o'clock is when it starts!"

"We don't want to be first though."

"Oh, God! No!" I completely agreed. Getting there first would be embarrassing, like just too eager, and specially if a boy arrived almost immediately afterwards and we were left on our own with him. I didn't know how to talk to boys! All very well Millie saying I'd got brothers, but you really *couldn't* count Coop or Fergus as boys.

"Best get there when there's other people so we can mingle," said Millie.

I said, "Yes! Mingle."

"'Cept not with Zoe and her mob."

"Yuck, no," I said. "Horrible!"

"Wouldn't mingle with them if they went on their bended knee and begged me."

"So who else is going to be there?" I said. "Do we know?"

"Halena? Brigid? Jolene? Not to mention *boys*!"

Millie giggled, so I giggled, too. It was like a kind of automatic reaction. Boys! Giggle, giggle.

"You don't think there'll be dancing?" I said.

"Dunno," said Millie.

"Cos I'm not sure I can dance!"

I waited for Millie to inform me, in her usual bracing fashion, that, "Anyone can dance. There's nothing to it." Instead she said, "Me neither!" She sounded a bit worried. It was only then that I realised: Millie was just as anxious as I was. It surprised me. Millie was always so sure of herself. Far more than me. But in spite of her confidence I knew that she sometimes still felt a bit of an outsider, what with being the only one in the class on a scholarship, and all the rest of us being what she called posh. It comforted me a little to know I wasn't the only one feeling apprehensive.

"Know what?" she said. "You should've asked Charlie."

I was puzzled. "Asked her what?"

"To show you how to dance! Then you could have shown me."

"She'd laugh," I said. "I mean, it's stupid! Everyone knows how to dance."

"'Cept us."

"God!" I said. "We're pathetic!"

But at least we could be pathetic together. I said this to Millie, and she agreed.

"We'll stick to each other like glue. Right?"

I said, "Right!"

I'd hoped that when the time grew near I'd be able to lurk in my room, spying out of the window until I saw Millie and her dad turn up, when I would instantly tear downstairs at the speed of light crying, "Mum, I'm off!" and get out of the house without anyone seeing me, and specially not Dad. In spite of everything, I still had pangs of guilt. Unfortunately, as I hurtled down the stairs I bumped slap bang into Flora, hurtling up.

"Your friend's here," she said.

"Thank you," I said. "I was aware."

"Just telling you," said Flora. "She's all dressed up in those trousers."

I was outraged. How did she know about the trousers? Honestly! You couldn't do *anything* in this family without everyone getting to hear about it. Unless it was something you wanted them to hear, like me and Ben training for the Paralympics, in which case they weren't interested.

"The ones you got her for the party?" said Flora. "I s'pose that's where you're off to. To the *party. I'm* going to Dad's birthday dinner. We're all going to Dad's birthday dinner. All of us except you. Poor Dad! What—"

"Why don't you just be quiet?" I said.

Flora gave a screech of laughter and scudded up the stairs on all fours. *Seriously* abnormal.

Dad was in the hall, hovering at the front door.

"I think your lift has arrived," he said. "I'll come and see you off."

I squirmed. "You don't have to."

"Don't be silly," said Dad. "Of course I do."

I did so hope he wasn't going to be rude. Well, not rude, exactly, but sometimes he can *say* things. Like if he was still offended by me choosing to go off with Millie and her dad instead of being at La Cigale with the rest of the family.

I needn't have worried. When he wants to, Dad can be quite charming. He said hello to Millie – he even managed to remember her name, which Mum never did – and he shook hands with her dad. He even thanked him for letting me stay the night, and told me and Millie to have a good time. Millie, in her special posh voice, said, "I do hope you enjoy your dinner."

Dad seemed amused. "I'm sure I shall," he said, and he waved cheerfully at us as we pulled away.

"Well!" Millie bounced round in the front seat to talk to me. "He didn't sound too cross."

Her dad chuckled. "You want to hear him on the radio, blasting away at people! I guess it's all part of the act, eh?"

I am never quite sure whether it is or it isn't, but I grinned reassuringly at Millie and agreed that Dad wasn't too cross. In fact, not really cross at all. It was Mum who had been so put out.

"So now all we've got to worry about – " Millie mouthed it at me – "is *boys*."

"I heard that," said her dad. "And I'm here to tell you it's one thing you *don't* have to worry about. Take it from me – the lads'll be far more scared of you than you are of them!"

"It's not that I'm *scared* of them," whispered Millie,

as we got out of the car. "It's just that I don't know what sort of things they like to talk about!"

"Football?" I said.

"Is that what Coop talks about?"

I said, "No, but you can't go by him."

"So what does *he* talk about?"

I stared at her, appalled. She really did fancy him!

"I mean, other than music?" she said. "He must talk about *something*."

I didn't have time to answer her as the front door was flung open and the Mouse stood there, beaming at us.

"Quick, quick," she said. "You're the last to arrive!"

She led the way down some steps to an enormous room in the basement. The boys, all six of them, were grouped together in a corner, the girls in little separate clusters dotted about. All except for Zoe, who was boldly talking to a boy who looked like an older version of the Mouse. Obviously her brother.

Millie clutched at my arm. "Stick like glue!"

We attached ourselves to one of the little clusters.

"Cool," said Brigid, nodding at Millie's trousers. Halena and Jolene both agreed.

"Where'd you get them?" said Halena.

"I..." Millie shot me a glance as if seeking approval. "A shop in the market?"

"Gina's," I said. I squeezed Millie's arm reassuringly. I wasn't going to spoil things for her. The others didn't need to know that my mum had paid for the trousers.

Everyone seemed to admire them. People kept coming over and saying how cool they were and asking where they'd come from. I wondered for a moment if perhaps I'd made a mistake. I should have bought the trousers for myself! But I couldn't really regret it, Millie was so happy.

"Hey!" Brigid nudged at me. "There's a boy over there keeps staring at you."

My head zipped round. I said, "Which boy?"

Brigid let out an anguished squeal. "You don't have to make it so obvious!"

"OK." I let my eyes glaze over, like I was simply lost in thought. "Tell me which one!"

"The one with the dark hair – DON'T LOOK!"

I said, "I'm not."

"I am," said Halena. She did so. "Phwoar!" She turned back, giggling. "GLD, man!"

"What are you talking about?" I said.

"Good-looking dude!"

And he was interested in *me*?

"He's still staring," said Millie. "Oh!" She gave a little squeak. "He's coming over!"

"Probably wants to talk to *you*," I muttered. Millie in her cool trousers. Which I could have been wearing!

"It's not me," said Millie. She gave me a sharp jab with her elbow. "It's you, dimbo!"

Omigod, it really was! He stood there in front of me, looking awkward, like he'd had to pluck up his courage to come over. I felt a bit awkward myself. I knew that everyone was watching, even if they were pretending not to.

"Excuse me, but are you Peaches McBride?" he said.

I swallowed and said yes. My heart was already sinking. Someone must have told him about Dad. He'd obviously come over to ask me for an autograph or an introduction. I waited for him to say how it was his big ambition to work in the media.

"I'm Zach," he said. I braced myself. "Zach Whitaker. I've got a little brother who's madly in love with you!"

Pardon me??? My face must have registered a total blank.

"Ben?" he said. "Christmas party? Paralympics?"

"*Oh*," I said. "*Ben!*"

Zach grinned. He seemed relieved that I remembered.

"He's been driving us nuts ever since. It's all he can talk about… his friend Beedth and the Baralim!"

He imitated the way his brother spoke, but he did it like he was really fond of him, not making fun.

"I'm really glad that he enjoyed it," I said. I had become aware that Millie and the others had discreetly melted away, leaving me on my own with Zach. I felt an embarrassed giggle bubbling up inside me and had to choke it back.

"Mum was ever so grateful," said Zach. "She was really worried in case things didn't work out. Ben doesn't always take to people. Like, if they can't understand him, or treat him like he's an idiot?"

"Oh, but he's not!" I said.

"It's what people think. Just because he can't talk properly."

I remembered the Mouse telling me how she found Ben difficult. "They don't try hard enough," I said. "You have to work at it. Like, just at first I couldn't properly understand him, but then after a while I got used to it and we had these really long conversations." Well, sort of conversations.

Zach grinned. "That's why he's fallen for you! Honestly, it's Beedth said this and Beedth said that and Beedth did it this way. He keeps nagging me to help with his training. He says he's going to be a *willcher adleed*."

"Wheelchair athlete!" I shouted it out triumphantly. Heads snapped round in my direction.

"I took him up the park the other day and he got all tetchy and impatient. Kept telling me how *Beedth* didn't do it that way! *Do like Beedth!*"

"All we did was just race up and down," I said. I giggled at the memory. "We nearly ran over Sister Agatha!"

"I know, he told me. He said you'd *rud owr a dud*."

"Run over a nun!" The heads whipped round again. Zach laughed.

"He was quite proud of it. But he seems to think you're going to be there with him, at the next Paralympics. He reckons you're going to race round together."

"What, with me pushing?"

"That's what he reckons."

"Oh." I could feel a frown crinkling my forehead. "P'raps I shouldn't have gone putting the idea into his head?"

"No, that's OK. He knows it's only a game. It's just that I obviously don't play it properly. Dunno what you did any different—"

"I just… raced him up and down," I said.

"Same here. But I'm not you! I don't suppose—" Zach hesitated. I wasn't sure, but I thought he might be blushing. It was hard to tell, cos he wasn't pale like me. When I blush I glow like a beacon. "I don't suppose you'd feel like coming to say hello to him some time?"

Help! Now he'd got me at it. Glowing like a beacon.

He obviously misread the signs. "Sorry," he mumbled. "Shouldn't have asked. I don't even know where you live. I'm just next door, but it's probably way too far for you to come."

"No," I said, "I'm quite near. I could get a bus."

Quickly he said, "You wouldn't have to do that. My mum could pick you up."

"Well, or my mum could give me a lift. But the bus is quite easy," I said. "I like going on buses."

"Yeah, me too," said Zach.

"My friend Millie," I said, "her dad's a bus driver."

I looked round for her, but she seemed to have vanished. And then I saw her, standing with Brigid. They were chatting happily with a couple of boys. So much for Millie saying she didn't know how to talk to them! Her new trousers must have given her confidence. But then I was also chatting happily to a boy. When I didn't stop to think about it and embarrass myself.

"That's Millie over there," I said. "I never used to go on buses till I met her. Now I do it all the time."

"It's nice to be independent, isn't it?" said Zach.

I agreed that it was. And then at that point we both came to a halt and didn't seem to know how to go on.

"Really," I said, "it wouldn't be any trouble coming by bus."

"If you did," said Zach, "I'd take you back home again afterwards."

I was doing my beacon act again. I could feel the waves of heat radiating off me.

"Oh, but you wouldn't have to do that," I said.

"I'd like to, though," said Zach.

There was a pause. We seem to have stopped again. I glowed madly.

"So—"

We both spoke at the same time.

"After you!"

Zach got in just ahead of me. I wished he hadn't cos I couldn't really think of anything to say. I opened my mouth and made a sort of *um* noise, like, "Um..."

"I've promised I'll take him up the park tomorrow," said Zach. "If the weather's OK."

"I could always come then, if you like," I said.

"Some time after lunch?"

"Any time," I said.

"'Bout two o'clock?"

"Two o'clock would be fine."

"D'you know which bus to get? There's one that stops just down the road. Number 19. Dunno if that goes near you?"

"I'll ask Millie's dad," I said. "He'll know. He knows every bus route there is."

"Wait till I tell Ben," said Zach. "He'll be so excited!"

CHAPTER TWELVE

It was nearly ten o'clock when we arrived back at Millie's place after the party. Millie's mum seemed slightly surprised that all we wanted to do was rush upstairs to Millie's bedroom.

"I thought you'd be all hyped," she said. "You can stay up later, you know! You don't have to go to bed for a while yet. Or maybe you're just wanting to be on your own to talk? Is that what it is?"

Millie's dad said, "Talk? They've been at it non-stop since we left! Chitter chatter, like a flock of starlings."

"And I dare say there's a lot more to come." Millie's mum nodded knowingly. "Likely they'll be wanting to pick over the bones."

"Dunno about bones," said Millie, as we raced helter-skelter up the stairs. "And you," she said, as one of the Diddy People put her head round a door, "you're supposed to be asleep!"

"Want to know about the party," said the Diddy Person. It was Kimberley, the littlest one.

"Tell you tomorrow," said Millie. "Me and Peachy have things to talk about."

"*Secrets.*"

"Yes, secrets! Nothing to do with you. Scram!"

We disappeared into Millie's room and flung ourselves down on the bed.

"So we *did* know how to dance!" I said.

"Yes, and I saw who you were dancing with," said Millie.

I said, "Yes, and I saw who *you* were dancing with!"

It was one of the boys that she and Brigid had been chatting to. Aaron, Millie said his name was. I couldn't help teasing her about it.

"Natter, natter, natter," I said. "Thought you didn't know how to talk to boys?"

"Thought *you* didn't," retorted Millie. "You and the Good-Looking Dude!"

I felt myself blushing, as usual. "He wanted to talk about Ben." I'd already told her that, in the car.

"Yeah, yeah," said Millie. "That's why he's asked you over!"

"It's only to see Ben," I said. "We're taking him up the park."

"Like he doesn't fancy you!" jeered Millie.

I protested that it was Ben who fancied me, not Zach.

"Wanna bet?" said Millie.

She made me promise to call her next day and report.

"So what happened?" she squealed when I rang her.

I said, "Well, I got the bus from Beechcroft Road, like your dad told me. The 24? It dropped me right near, so—"

"*But what happened?* When you got there?"

"We took Ben up the park and practised for the Paralympics."

"Is that all?"

"Well, and we talked a bit."

"About what?"

"I dunno. Just… things."

"So then what happened?"

"Then we took Ben home and Zach came back on the bus with me."

"What, all the way?"

"Yes."

"Hah!"

What did she mean, *hah?*

"Did you invite him in?"

I said, "No, he had to get home. His gran was coming."

"Oh."

There was a silence, while she thought about it. In the end I had to put her out of her misery.

"I'm going to see him again next week," I said. "After we've broken up."

"Hah!" said Millie.

"I'm going to go and say hello to Ben first and then we're going into town to do some Christmas shopping."

"Do boys do that sort of thing?" said Millie.

"Dunno," I said.

"I don't think they do! He's only doing it cos he fancies you."

"What about you and Aaron?" I said.

"Don't change the subject!"

"Has he called you yet?" She'd said that he might be going to.

"Yes," said Millie. "If you must know."

I said, "If you insist on hearing about me and Zach, it's only fair I hear about you and Aaron."

"'There's nothing to hear!"

"*Yet*," I said.

Nobody at home knew that I was seeing Zach. I told Mum that I was going to visit Ben.

"You know? The boy I looked after at the Christmas party?"

"Oh, yes," said Mum. She clearly didn't remember. "That's nice of you! Just take care you don't make a rod for your own back."

"What's that mean?" I said.

"Try not to give him too much encouragement. You don't want him thinking you're always at his beck and call."

I said, "*Mum!* I'm doing it cos I *want* to."

There were times when Mum just didn't get it.

Christmas came and went, and then Dad's New Year bash, which I normally dreaded. Somehow, this time, it wasn't so bad. I didn't drop anything, or spill anything – last year I'd had a complete disaster on both counts – and I actually managed to talk to people without getting all tongue-tied and embarrassed, which is something that has always driven Mum and Dad half demented. That a daughter of theirs couldn't *communicate*, for goodness sake!

The day before we went back to school Dad decided that we must all go out for an end-of-holiday meal.

"Let's have an Indian! We haven't had an Indian for ages."

We drove into town and Dad dropped us off outside the restaurant – his favourite, as usual, the Star of Bengal – while he went to find a parking space. Raj came to greet us, full of smiles, wondering why he hadn't seen us for so long. At the tops of their voices, Mum and Charlie, Coop and the twins, all started to explain. I was about to trail after them across the restaurant, when I was stopped by a joyous cry of "Beeeeedth!" I turned and saw Ben, in his wheelchair. He was with his mum and dad, and Zach. Zach grinned and waved. I immediately went over to say hello.

We talked for a bit, mainly me and Ben, cos he was so excited at seeing me, until his mum told him to 'Let Peachy go now, and get her dinner'.

"See you at the weekend?" I said. "Go up the park?"

"Baralim!" shouted Ben.

As I turned to go, Zach swivelled round on his chair. "I'll come and pick you up."

"You don't have to," I said.

"But I want to."

I said, "Oh. Well! OK, then. I'll see you!"

"See you," said Zach.

I reached our table to find Charlie craning her head, trying to see who I'd been talking to.

"Who was *that?*" she said.

"Just someone I know," I said.

"But who is he?"

"His name's Zach."

"*Zach.*" She nodded approvingly. "Cool!"

"Is he your boyfriend?" said Flora.

"None of your business," I said.

"But I want to know!"

"So do I," said Fergus.

"Both of us want to!"

"*Is* he?" said Charlie.

"He's very good-looking," said Mum, in tones of some surprise.

"Boyfriend, boyfriend, boyfriend!" chanted Charlie. "Is he or isn't he?"

"What's all the racket?" said Dad, taking his seat. "What's going on?"

"It's just Peachy," said Flora. "She's been talking to a boy and she won't tell us whether he's her boyfriend or not."

"Oh, is that all?" said Dad, immediately losing interest. "I thought perhaps it was something important."

Charlie rolled her eyes at me across the table. I rolled mine back.

"I saw that," said Dad. "Stop ganging up on me!"

I had never ganged up with Charlie on anyone before, and specially not on Dad. Now, suddenly, it seemed like we were banded together in the face of male stupidity. Saying that boyfriends weren't important!

"I shall find out," warned Charlie.

"So shall I," said Flora.

"Oh, darling, do tell!" said Mum. "Is he or isn't he? We're all desperate to know!"

Coop groaned. "All this luvvy-duvvy stuff!"

"You keep out of it," said Charlie. "This is between us and Peachy. Nothing to do with you."

"Oh, leave them to it," said Dad. "I'm going to order my food."

"Me too," I said. "I'm starving!"

I reached out for a menu.

"You needn't think you're getting away that easily," said Charlie. "I intend to go on nagging!"

"You can nag as much as you like," I said. "I'm going to have prawn biryani."

As Raj came to take the orders I remembered how we had all sat here at this very table, way back, almost a year before. I had tried so hard to make myself heard! I had shouted, **"FIRE!"** (in a manner of speaking) in this really LOUD voice, and still nobody had paid any attention. *And* they had all ordered their food and forgotten I even existed. *And* Mum and Dad had pinched the best bits of chicken off my plate.

I beamed up at Raj. "I'll have a prawn biryani, please. And do we want poppadoms?"

"Oh, I think so," said Mum.

"And six p—"

"Eight," said Dad.

"Eight poppadoms."

"Spicy ones!" shrieked Flora. "I want spicy ones!"

"You don't like them," said Mum.

"I do so!"

"No, you don't," said Coop. "Last time you had one you spat it out."

"That was *last* time. This is *this* time."

"Give us spicy ones!" roared Fergus.

Mum and I exchanged glances. Mum gave a little shrug of the shoulders. I turned back to Raj.

"Six plain, please, and two spicy."

"They won't eat them," said Charlie.

"Too bad," said Dad. "They've made their choice, they can stick with it."

"You needn't think you're going to have any of mine," said Coop.

"Don't want any of yours!"

"Just as well, cos you're not getting any."

"Mum, what are you going to have?" I said.

"I think I'll have… what is it you're having?"

"Prawn biryani."

"That sounds good. I'll have the same."

"Dad?"

"Give me a minute, give me a minute," grumbled Dad. "I haven't decided."

"*Duck*," said Flora. "I want duck!"

"There isn't any duck," I said.

"Peking duck!"

"That's Chinese," said Charlie witheringly.

Flora said, "Oh."

"Choose something else."

"Like what?"

"Anything," I said. "Just get on with it."

"Roast beef!" bellowed Fergus.

"Haggis!" shouted Flora. They both collapsed into giggles.

"If you two don't stop messing around," said Mum, "you can just have your spicy poppadoms and a glass of water."

"Then you'll be sorry," I said.

The talk swirled on, taking me with it. Across the room Zach caught my eye.

"See you Saturday," he mouthed.

Charlie gave an exultant shriek. "Gotcha!" she cried.

"What?" said Coop.

"He *is* her boyfriend!"

"Peachy's got a boyfriend, Peachy's got a boyfriend!" Flora chanted, drumming on the table with both hands. Fergus immediately joined in.

"Peachy's got a—"

"Just button it," I said. But I must admit, I said it rather feebly. It seemed I didn't have to shout any more. I'd got everyone's attention just speaking normally. Well, everyone's except Dad's. He was still earnestly studying his menu.

"Chicken tikka," he announced, in tones of deep satisfaction. "I shall have chicken tikka." He took off his glasses and gazed round benevolently at the rest of us. "What's going on? Am I missing something?"

"Oh, Alastair, for heaven's sake!" said Mum.

"What?" said Dad. "What?"

Charlie looked at me across the table. Sadly she shook her head.

"Honestly," she said. "Not a clue!"

More fantastic reads from Jean Ure...

LEMONADE SKY

When Ruby's Mum disappears, Ruby takes
charge – Mum's left her and her two sisters
alone before. But will they be OK? And can
they keep Mum's disappearance a secret until
she gets back?

More fantastic reads from Jean Ure...

ICE LOLLY

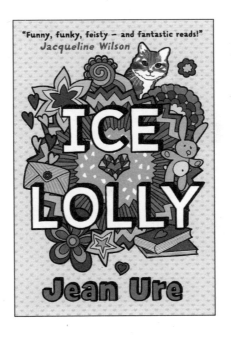

Without Mum, everything is just so *hard*.
Things would be easier if I could just stop
feeling; if I could just freeze, like an ice lolly...

More fantastic reads from Jean Ure...

SKINNY MELON AND ME

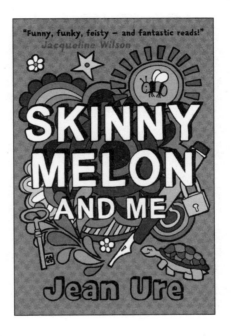

This is the diary of Cherry Louise Waterton.

Problem One: My mum's just remarried a total
dweeb named Roland Butter.

Problem Two: I think she has a secret too...